# UNDER THE
# DUSTY MOON

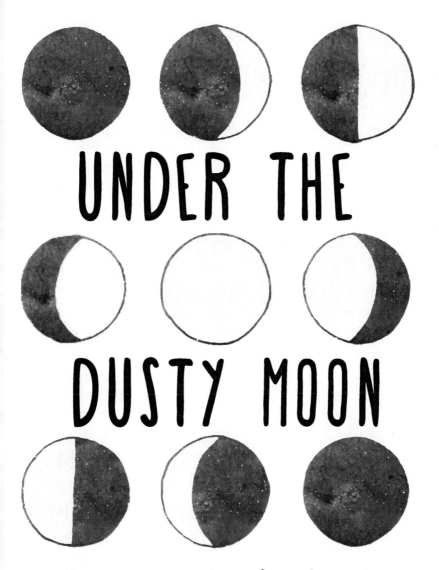

# UNDER THE

# DUSTY MOON

Suzanne Sutherland

DUNDURN
TORONTO

Editor: Shannon Whibbs
Design: Laura Boyle
Cover Design: Laura Boyle
Cover Image: © runLenarun/shutterstock.com
Printer: Webcom

**Library and Archives Canada Cataloguing in Publication**

Sutherland, Suzanne, 1987-, author
        Under the dusty moon / Suzanne Sutherland.

Issued in print and electronic formats.
ISBN 978-1-4597-3202-5 (paperback).--ISBN 978-1-4597-3203-2 (pdf).--
ISBN 978-1-4597-3204-9 (epub)

        I. Title.

PS8637.U865U54 2016          jC813'.6          C2015-904181-3
                                               C2015-904182-1

1   2   3   4   5      20   19   18   17   16

  Canada

We acknowledge the support of the **Canada Council for the Arts** and the **Ontario Arts Council** for our publishing program. We also acknowledge the financial support of the **Government of Canada** through the **Canada Book Fund** and **Livres Canada Books**, and the **Government of Ontario** through the **Ontario Book Publishing Tax Credit** and the **Ontario Media Development Corporation**.

**Visit us at**

Dundurn.com | @dundurnpress | Facebook.com/dundurnpress | Pinterest.com/dundurnpress

Dundurn
3 Church Street, Suite 500
Toronto, Ontario, Canada
M5E 1M2

*For Graham and his Strange Powers*

# One

There's this huge all-day concert that happens on the Island at the end of every summer. You have to take a ferry across the lake just to get there, but it feels like practically the whole city goes.

We went last year, Mom and me. The crowd was unreal, this swarming mass of tattoos and band shirts, Keds and sunglasses. If you turned away from the crowd, you could see all the giant office buildings and high-rise condos of Toronto's gap-toothed skyline casting their reflections across Lake Ontario, but if you faced the stage, you were completely surrounded by the sound and the sky and the sweaty, sunburned crowd.

It was amazing.

And this year they asked Mom to play.

I got all excited when she told me, even though it's totally not like me to flip every time she books a show. When I'd finished geeking out, I was dumb enough to ask her if she thought that this was going to be her big break as a solo act, but she just laughed.

It was kind of a sad laugh, really. And she shook her head. Her thick brown hair swung side to side in that easy way that it does. There's more grey in it these days, but she still looks like a kid. My hair doesn't swing that way, that shampoo-commercial way that hers does, it just hangs there, limp, like it can't be bothered to move.

"Aw, sweets," she said, ruffling my dirty-blond mop, "you know it's not really about breaks. You just keep on working."

"Yeah, I know," I said, already embarrassed by my enthusiasm. "But you're still going to play the fest, right?"

"Of course. I'll keep singing as long as they keep calling me back for more. But you know how it is, just another day at the office."

"Uh huh," I said, "I know."

Micky Wayne is my mom.

She isn't famous, but she used to be. "Canadian-famous," I heard someone call her once. Or maybe I read it. I can't remember. People write about her a lot. Or they used to, anyway.

She's a musician: a singer and a guitar player. Sometimes she plays with a band and sometimes she just plays on her own. She used to sing in a band called Dusty Moon, and they were really popular before they broke up. Now she mostly just plays her own songs.

People know her name. And because they know her name, some people even know mine. Not that they know anything about me, or even what I look like, but they know whole songs about me. They know that daisies are my favourite flower, and that my mom calls me Vic, even though she's the only one who's allowed to. I'm Victoria to everyone else. And I'm definitely not Vicky, to anyone. For obvious reasons. Sometimes I think that Mom chose a rhyming name for me on purpose. She's always wanted us to be like sisters, like twins, when really we're total opposites. But I guess she is my best friend, even though I'd never admit it to her.

When I was born, Mom was still on the road a lot with Dusty Moon. And more than anything she wanted to be a mom, but more than anything she also wanted to play music. She's never been particularly decisive. So for a while she tried to balance the two; not that I remember, but there are hours of footage of me toddling around Dusty Moon's tour bus and crying about having to wear my noise-cancelling headphones that looked like giant plastic earmuffs when the band played shows.

I guess it must've been pretty hard, even though she had a tour nanny to help her most of the time. She never looks very happy in those videos from when I was little, just exhausted. She wasn't sure that she was doing the right thing by bringing me with her, by continuing to tour, but playing music was the only job she'd ever had. She didn't know how to do anything else. And as much as they loved me, the rest of the band wasn't super thrilled that I was always there with them. It kind of tore her up, I think. I mean, she never talks about it, but she wrote about it in a whole bunch of songs, the first ones she wrote for her to sing on her own. They make up most of her first solo album. She wrote them because she didn't know what to do and she felt stuck. But then the choice kind of got made for her.

She's been back on the road a little bit in the last couple of years as a solo act, finally getting to play the songs that she stored up for so long. It's easier now that I'm old enough to be left mostly alone while she's gone. It's usually just weekends out of town, though, nothing as major as before. She plays a few old Dusty Moon songs in her sets, but it's mostly stuff that's just hers.

Mom's songs are pretty personal. Like, show-up-to-school-naked-like-in-a-dream-but-it's-not-actually-a-dream kind of personal, which is a genre I'm pretty sure she made up. I'd shrivel up like a sideshow shrunken head if people knew half as much about me as they do about her, but she just puts it all out there: her loneliness and her desire and her frustrations. It's embarrassing sometimes, but there's not much I can do about it. That's just who she is: transparent. Her heart's not so much on her sleeve as it is set out on a plate that she's passing around the crowd for everyone to take a bite of.

Anyway, it was the middle of July when Mom found out about the concert on the Island. During the kind of sticky, stinky summer heat wave that makes you feel like you're living in someone's armpit. I stayed inside as much as I could, and even though our air conditioner was seriously on its last legs it was still better than being outside.

After Mom made her big Island announcement, she had to leave for band practice. She zipped her acoustic-electric guitar into its bag and slipped the straps over her shoulders like a backpack. Then she picked up her bike and carried it down the stairs; she was almost able to make a tricky manoeuvre like that look graceful.

"I'll be back in time for dinner, okay?" she called back over her shoulder.

"Yeah," I said, "if you don't get fried alive out there."

I texted Luce to see if she wanted to come over. She texted back a minute later to say she'd be right there, and what colour freezie did I want.

*You know me*, I texted, *true blue.*

*Obviously.*

Lucy's parents own a convenience store, the one at the end of our street, and that's how we first met. This was just after we'd moved Toronto, a little over three years ago. When Mom realized that if she wanted to get back to playing music and touring like an actual working musician we might have to move to a slightly bigger city. And to be closer to the one person she could count on to look after me while she was out of town: her mother, who'd moved to Toronto after my grampa died. We'd been living in Moncton before that, and in Halifax, with Gran and Grampa, when I was little. Mom used to joke that I'd have my first cross-Canada tour under my belt by the time I turned eighteen. I told her she might want to work on her standup routine before she started working the comedy-club circuit.

So we'd found a new apartment, a tiny little two-bedroom with perma-dirty linoleum floors and an inexplicably large closet that Mom said would be perfect for a mini-studio. She signed the lease on the spot, while our new landlord talked excitedly into his Bluetooth in what sounded like Portuguese. The apartment was in Parkdale, which meant it wasn't all that far away from Gran's house, so dirt aside, it seemed pretty ideal.

Gran and I don't get along super well, but she's okay. Most of the time. Even when I was a little kid we never exactly got each other. Grampa, when he was alive, did the translating for both of us, and without him things didn't really work. I was really sad after he died, but Mom was worse. She stopped writing songs, barely left the house, and she and Gran fought all the time. Which I guess is why Gran decided to pack up and leave Halifax. We left not too long after that and found a place in Moncton. For a while Mom and Gran weren't even speaking, but eventually they got over it. Still, after thirteen years of living on the other side of the country from her, it seemed pretty weird to be moving so we could be close to someone I hardly knew.

We'd driven Mom's van — The Grimace, it's big and purple like that old McDonald's character — all the way from Nova Scotia to Ontario with all of our stuff in the back. Well, not quite all of it, some of it was being shipped over after us. But the shipment was delayed, so for about a week we were just squatting in the new place with no furniture or anything, just stacks of boxes and old milk crates. And Mom was so exhausted from the drive and the unpacking we'd done when we arrived that she squeezed my shoulders and whispered in my ear, "What do you say we go lazy shopping?" Which is what she calls it when she's too tired to go to an actual grocery store and we shop at the closest corner store instead.

So we trooped down the flight of stairs from our apartment to the street. And she took my hand in hers and we went inside the first little shop we found. She was wearing an old band shirt stretched at the seams, and she stunk of sweat from the long drive. I had insisted on her buying me real deodorant — not the hippie crystal stuff that she used — ever since I was old enough to need it. I was frazzled and frayed, but at least I smelled all right.

"Lynn's Convenience," Mom whispered as we passed through the door. "Oh, look, Vic, we chose right." She pointed to a fat, orange tabby cat that was prowling near the potato-chip rack. Mom is such a cat lady, she loses her mind around anything with pointy ears and whiskers, even though she's allergic and we can't actually have one in our place. Within seconds she was down on her knees, tickling this strange cat behind the ears and baby-talking like there was no one else around to hear her.

"Oh, what a handsome boy you are. Yes, yes, yes, so handsome. Such a beautiful, beautiful boy."

I was used to this kind of performance, but it was still mortifying to see her go totally gaga in public. My face flushed hot and red, and I made my way to the back of the store to find a distraction in the form of some chocolate milk. That was when I first saw Lucy, sitting on a folding chair with a mini DVD player propped up on the counter in front of her. She'd stopped

13

paying attention to whatever movie she'd been watching, though, and was full-on staring at Mom losing her mind over the cat, just barely containing her laughter. I gave her a dirty look, even though I knew exactly how ridiculous Mom looked. I grabbed the chocolate milk, along with a carton of plain two-percent for Mom, plus three boxes of Kraft Dinner and a packet of Mr. Noodles, nearly dropping everything as I walked back to the front of the store, cradling our loot in my arms.

"What's your hurry, love?" Mom asked, still enraptured with the cat. "This is Felix, isn't he gorgeous?" She finally broke her loving gaze and surveyed my haul. "Let's see, three boxes of Kraft Dinner? Hmm, we're going to need some butter, too. And let's grab some cheese and a loaf of bread, and, oh, let's get some microwave popcorn, too. And some Diet Coke."

I unloaded my bounty onto the counter and the two of us went hunting for the rest of the items on the shopping list that only existed in her head. When we'd grabbed enough of what she deemed real food, the man behind the counter started ringing us up. Our lazy shopping trip turned out to be pretty substantial, and the man behind the cash register called for the girl at the back to come help him. And Mom, being Mom, just went for it.

"Hey," she said, taking me by the shoulders and pointing me toward the girl, "this is Victoria. What's your name?"

"Lucy," her father supplied, while the girl kept her head down, stuffing our first Toronto meal into thin grey-green plastic bags. "My name is Walter."

"Hi, Walter. Lucy, you and Vic must be about the same age. What grade are you in?"

If my face had been red before from Mom carrying on with the cat, I was a glowing stop sign now.

"Seven," she said.

"Oh, wow, Vic's just about to start grade eight at the school down the street here. Is that your school, too?"

"Yeah," she said.

"Isn't that great, Vic?

"Mm-hmm," I said, studying the chocolate bars on the shelves below the counter. "Great."

"It's thirty-six forty-nine all together," Lucy's dad said. No one in the history of the world has ever been able to spend as much money at convenience stores as Mom and I do.

"Perfect," Mom said, "perfect," while she dug into the pockets of her jeans for the folded up twenties she'd tucked in before we left. She handed them over, collected her change, and we took our bags from the counter.

"Bye, Walter! Bye, Lucy! Bye, Felix!" she called back as we left.

Micky Wayne, a one-woman welcome wagon. It was so humiliating.

"Why did you do that?" I whisper-yelled, smacking her arm with the back of my free hand as soon as we'd walked past the store window.

"Ow, ow, you're hurting me," she whined. "Stop it, Vic, you're too strong!"

"I hate you," I hissed, smacking her again. "You never take anything I say seriously."

"Please," she said, "no more, I can't take it! It hurts!"

"Mom!"

And we carried on like that all the way back up the stairs and into our new home. As we started unpacking the food, I tried again.

"You can't do that to me, you know. I don't need you to make friends for me."

"I know," she said begrudgingly.

"Say it," I insisted. "Say the whole thing."

"I know that you're old enough to make your own friends."

"Do you actually?" I asked.

"You're old enough to make Kraft Dinner all by yourself and you're old enough to make your own friends," she recited robotically.

"Exactly," I said, over-enunciating my words, "and I would thank you to remember that."

"And old enough to make a liquor-store run for me?" she asked, wiggling her shoulders.

"I wish."

"Me, too. I'm just going to pop out and get some wine, okay? Do you mind starting dinner?"

"I thought you said we were getting a personal chef when we moved to Toronto," I said, searching through a stack of boxes for one marked KITCHEN.

"Is that what you heard me say?" she asked. "I told you we were getting a personal ... shelf."

"Weak, Mom."

"I know," she said, tapping her head. "Mama needs her brain juice."

"So go on, then."

"Okay. See you soon, sweets."

Luce came over with the freezies and I picked up where I'd left off my game of *Lore of Ages V*. It's actually Lucy's game, but she's been lending me the series, one by one, since she first got me into it last year. You play as Stara Shah, a time-travelling adventurer and all around kick-ass lady. Each game is different, but they're all about saving an ancient civilization from disappearing, which you do by collecting their artifacts and stories, and sometimes you have to fight one of their gods in the process. Other than in the first game, where she's dressed kind of plain, Stara always wears her signature knee-high red boots, black pants, and red leather jacket, with a tattoo of an eagle on her chest and a jet-black high ponytail that reaches all the way down to her waist. It's, like, a perfect outfit, and I've been trying to find a pair of boots like Stara's for months.

We had to download old system emulators onto Mom's and my computer to play the first few of them. They came out before Lucy and I were even born, and they look all funny and pixelated. Lucy's beaten the whole series already, at least until *Lore of Ages VI* comes out in the fall, but she's been coaching me while I play through it. She swears that her love of *Lore of Ages* — *LoA* to its most devoted players — is so deep that she actually loves watching me stumble my way through it, but sometimes I think she's just mining my goofy screw-ups for her fanfiction.

Lucy spends a lot of time online talking to other people who are into *LoA* and the other games she plays. Sometimes we'll go on the forums together at her house, but I never have much to say on my own. Lucy's made some good friends through the game, though, and through her fanfiction. They seem really cool, but when we all chat together I kind of feel like a tourist.

Word is that there's going to be a playable demo of *LoA VI* at Fan Con this year, this big convention that happens at the end of the summer. Lucy and I had been planning to go together, but when I told Mom how much the four-day convention pass cost, she nearly did a spit-take. Lucy was pissed at me when I told her I couldn't go, but made plans to meet up with some of her friends from the forums instead, which made me feel totally left out.

Lately I've been working on my fanart — even though I haven't let anyone else see it. I've been trying to draw this portrait of Stara, but I can never get her face just right: her high arched eyebrows, tawny brown skin, and her perfect little smirk. I can see it perfectly in my head, but it never comes out looking that way on paper. Still, I keep on trying. Eventually I might get it right.

"Okay, hold on. Can I just, like, suggest something here?" Lucy asked, when I'd been playing for less than a minute.

"Oh, come on," I said, "I thought I was doing okay!"

"Well, yeah," she said, "you are. Just, you could be doing a lot more okay, you know? You've got to check under that rock over there. You see it?"

"Oh, right," I said, moving the rock and finding a gem that was hidden underneath.

"Right," she said, "you've got it. Now keep on walking."

I paused the game, already looking for an excuse to talk about something else. Lucy's great, but she doesn't realize how much of a control freak she can be when she's watching me play one of her games. "You think I should ask Shaun to hang out?" I said.

"Who's Shaun?" she asked, taking the end of her purple freezie out of her mouth.

"You know, that guy from my drama class. I told you about him."

"Oh," she said. "Why?"

"I told you, he's kind of cool. We did that project together that time. I just, I don't know, feel like actually making something happen this summer, you know?"

"Well, yeah," Lucy said, biting off the tip of her freezie and chomping on the purple ice. "But why do you like him?"

It was a fair question. Why did I like Shaun?

Shaun with his pudgy cheeks and his shaggy red hair. He had this sheepish grin whenever he rolled in late to class with some flimsy excuse, which was almost every day, reeking of weed, with those baby-blue bloodshot eyes. Shaun, who was actually taller than me, who didn't make me feel like a freak when I stood next to him. Who wrote made-up inspirational quotes on the board whenever our teachers were late for class. "Never stop believing in your winged dreams of tomorrow. Forever and ever, ape men."

What wasn't to like?

My real plan for that day had been to ask Shaun to go to the Island with me, but Mom's big announcement had thrown me off my game, though I wasn't really sure why.

The Island seemed like an innocent enough idea, kind of nostalgic, so maybe he wouldn't notice how terrified I was of asking him out. Which wasn't even a thing people really did anymore, but it sounded so classic and cool. Cheesy in just the right way. The ferry dock was only a short bike ride away from our neighbourhood. I figured I could smuggle out some of Mom's rum, maybe mix it with some orange juice and bust out my new mint-green-and-gold bikini.

I wanted to do it really old school, go over to his house and then just happen to pass by while he was out mowing the lawn with his shirt off, like in an Archie comic or a corny teen movie. I'd casually mention that I was thinking of heading over to the Island for the afternoon, and, oh, did he want to come along? Cool, yeah, no problem. Let's do it.

And every step and every word would play out perfectly. We'd go to the beach, fall madly in love, and have sex in the strategically camouflaged sand dunes. The way it only ever happens in romance novels or particularly steamy fanfiction. I knew it wasn't real life, but that didn't stop me from wanting it.

I admit that I had some of Mom's stories, the ones that really happened to her, buzzing in my ear while I dreamed the whole unnecessarily elaborate thing up. Like when, after hours of begging, she told me the story of the time she lost her virginity. She was fifteen, and she and her boyfriend had hitchhiked to the beach. They brought a bottle of Grampa's homemade wine and made love (her words) in an abandoned lifeguard station nearby. Her boyfriend made a giant heart in the sand out of the blue and purple stones all around them, and they fell asleep together, just like that.

I didn't tell Luce about it, though. We don't talk about guys very much. Like, at all. She hates it when I bring up stuff like that. I don't know why, but she just never seems to want to hear about it.

So I told her never mind, I didn't mean it about asking Shaun out and we went back to it, me playing the game and Lucy offering encouragement that veered dangerously close to spoiler territory. Eventually she had to leave to help her parents close the store. I turned the game off and pulled out my sketchbook, trying to draw Stara's nose right for the hundredth time. I ruined it by making the tiny bump in the bridge too big and then accidentally ripped through the paper trying to erase my mistake. I tore the evidence out of my sketchbook and made a pile of confetti with it on my bed. I stirred a finger through the pieces and then threw it all in the garbage. Was it possible I was getting worse?

Mom came back from practice an hour after that. I heard her struggling to get her bike back up the stairs and muted the TV show I had on.

"What's for dinner, sweets?" Mom called as she opened the door. "I'm starving."

I glanced at the old clock hanging on the wall, something Mom picked up at Goodwill. It had a bird by each number and made cheesy bird calls every hour. It was just after eight. My stomach gurgled, as if on cue.

"I thought you were cooking tonight," I said, my eyes back on the TV.

"Hi, I'm Micky. Have we met?" she stood in front of me, blocking my view.

I hit pause again. "Aren't you some huge rock star?"

"You must be thinking of someone else," she said, plunking herself down next to me on the couch.

"Oh." Unpaused. "Right. Who are you, again?"

"No idea. So, what, then … pizza?"

"Not pizza. Chinese?" I countered.

"Nah, Mel and I wound up in Chinatown last night. I OD'd on dumplings and cold tea."

Mel, her bassist, was ten years younger than her and was always trying to drag Mom out to bars and after-hours clubs. Cold tea, I knew, was a code that some of the restaurants in Chinatown used. If you ordered cold tea after the bars had stopped serving, they'd sell you beer in a teapot. Mel had been a big fan of Dusty Moon when she was younger, but had auditioned to be in Mom's backing band a few years ago and slayed the competition. Mostly Mom was immune to her persuasion, but sometimes she gave in.

"Hello, TMZ?" I said, grabbing my phone.

"I wish," she said, flipping her hair over her shoulder and striking an exaggerated pose.

"You don't."

"True," she said, and stopped her voguing. "Thai?"

"Kensington?"

"Hungary Thai it is."

# Two

As if that wasn't where we wound up for dinner at least once a week, anyway. The restaurant was half Hungarian and half Thai food, as the name might suggest, and we practically had our own table there. Their menu was a surprisingly perfect combination for Mom and me, since we almost never craved the same foods at the same time.

Mom quickly got changed and I tossed my phone into my bag and we walked up to Dundas to catch the streetcar. My stomach was singing gurgly protest songs the whole way up as our flip-flops smacked against the sidewalk in unison and then out again. Mom had changed back into the same shirt — a stretched-out and faded polka-dot tank — that she'd been wearing for a couple of days, which was a bad habit she fell into anytime she was really busy or stressed out. I noticed a faded mustard stain near her left boob as we walked, but was pretty sure that she hadn't, even if it was days-old. I used to think that she dressed this way on purpose, almost obnoxiously un-put-together, but eventually I figured out it was just that she couldn't bring herself to care about how she looked. She overcompensates for dressing like a slob by piling on the accessories. Some days you can hear her coming from a block away because she's wearing all of her bangles at once, but that's only on days that she doesn't have band practice. She doesn't wear jewellery at all when she's heading to practice, but the half sleeve of tattoos on her upper right arm dresses up her otherwise bland band uniform of a plain white V-neck and black jeans. She wears the exact same outfit to every practice, even in winter. Her tattoos make it look cool, though: flowers of every colour, shape, and size crowding her skin make her look like a walking garden.

The funny thing was that even without trying, Mom could still totally make a spread in some too-cool fashion magazine. With her teeth and her hair unbrushed. Fly-away greys and all. It's just who she is.

When the streetcar arrived we walked through the car and grabbed a double seat toward the back. I thought I saw a girl with pink Wayfarer sunglasses and chunky bangs staring at us as we walked by.

*Sorry*, I thought, *nothing to see here. Just Micky Wayne and her not-so-little sidekick. Move along, move along.*

Eventually the streetcar made it to Denison, so I pulled the little string dinger and the driver let us off. We walked up Augusta Avenue and into the market — Kensington Market, the city's hippie mecca. The streets were small but crammed with fruit markets, coffee shops, and second-hand clothing stores, and somehow the whole neighbourhood smelled like cinnamon. On a warm summer night the place was full of people, smiling as they passed each other on the sidewalk, or else forgetting the sidewalk altogether and walking in the middle of the road because there were so few cars driving through. The park we passed as we walked north on Augusta was full of kids that didn't look much older than me, playing hand drums and dancing with balls of fire swinging from a chain. The first time I saw it — poi, I think it's called — I asked Mom if she'd let me try.

"You're kidding, right?" she'd said. "I've seen you burn yourself on incense."

"Only twice," I protested, but that was the end of the discussion.

The restaurant was just north of the park, so we managed to make it there before either one of us collapsed from hunger. We nabbed our usual spot on the patio and Mom and I ordered automatically — schnitzel for me, lemongrass chicken and a glass of white wine for her — from a man who offered us a familiar smile. I was embarrassed because he was the one who'd served us the last two times we were there. Plus, you know, he was gorgeous. Like, your-kid-brother's-camp-counsellor-gorgeous. If I had a kid brother. This dude had a sort of sporty-meets-earthy style — he had little spacers in his earlobes that looked like they were made out of bamboo. Total hippie. But, I mean, almost everyone in Kensington was a granola-muncher of some kind.

The waiter had just left when Mom's and my phones buzzed simultaneously. We exchanged apologetic looks, a rare truly twinned moment for us, as we flexed our lower lips outwards and shrugged our shoulders. There were a few of Mom's expressions that were burned into my DNA. No matter where I went or who I became, I'd always have that Micky Wayne face when my phone went off at the wrong time. It was probably going to follow me to a job interview one day, and, knowing Mom's luck with employment, would cost me the gig.

I looked at my phone's display: new message from SHAUN.

*What, seriously? No. Way.*

I glanced at Mom, who seemed unimpressed by her caller. Her agent, probably.

She picked up, and I turned off the vibration alert on my phone before taking a quick breath and then opening Shaun's text.

"Hey, John," Mom said, "how are you?" And then her voice kind of faded into the background.

*Who is this?* the message said.

*You texted me*, I tapped out on my phone's keypad, before adding, *it's Victoria.*

*Oh yeah. You gave me your number that time*, he texted back almost instantaneously. It was a little freaky how quickly he fired off his messages. *The time we worked on that thing.*

*Yeah*, I texted, *drama class.* I blanked. It felt like there was a hummingbird in my chest fighting for its escape.

*So*, I cleared my throat, thankful that Shaun couldn't tell over text, *how's it going?*

*Good. Yeah. Just couldn't remember who I put in my phone under this name.*

*What name?* The hummingbird coughed and sputtered and then started doing somersaults.

*You're gonna laugh.*

*No way*, I texted. *Tell me.* Was this a thing? Him giving me a nickname when we'd barely even spoken outside of class? Did he even know what my last name was?

*No for real.*

*Just tell me!*

And then, from some tiny part of my brain that wasn't working overtime trying to process this unbelievable conversation with Shaun, I heard Mom say, "Wow. I've never played there before."

The hummingbird stopped dead.

*Big V.*

Not exactly the cute nickname I'd had in mind, but it was appropriate enough. The dead hummingbird felt like a ten-pound barbell.

"Look," Mom said, her voice fading back in, "can I call you tomorrow so we can figure the rest of this out? I'm out for dinner with Vic and —"

*Anyway*, Shaun texted, *maybe I'll see you around or something.*

*Do you want to —* I watched my thumb tap out before my brain had a chance to stop it.

"Okay, I will," said Mom. "Bye."

*— go to the Island sometime?*

Mom switched her phone off and put it back in her bag as I stared unblinking at my conversation with Shaun. Was this happening?

Mom took a sip from her wineglass and looked down the street toward the park before turning back to me with her *put-down-the-phone-already* look just as a new message popped up on my screen.

*Yeah*, Shaun texted, *cool.*

Putting my phone back into my bag felt like reaching the finish line of the Tour de France. My legs were useless and rubbery, and my right hand was actually trembling.

"Who was that?" Mom asked, grabbing at my shaking hand like she was an anxious kindergartner and not the woman who gave birth to me.

"A guy," I volleyed, suddenly pretending to be very interested in my glass of water. "What did John want?"

"I asked first," she insisted.

"So? Your thing is actually important career-stuff. Mine is just …"

"Just what?" she asked, her eyes nearly doubling in size.

"Just a guy. Guy-stuff."

"What guy?" Mom asked, clutching at my hand.

"You're relentless."

"Thank you." She bowed in her little plastic chair.

"That wasn't a compliment."

"Clearly." She rolled her eyes. No one rolls their eyes. My mom is the only human on the planet who actually does it, and it is unbelievably irritating.

I stared her down, arms crossed over my chest.

"Tell me!" she squealed, waving her hands in front of me.

I sighed. Audibly. A big cartoony sigh. This is not what mothers are supposed to act like. It's ridiculous. People were staring at us. But the only way to shut her up, I knew, was to give her information. In my tiniest voice, I admitted, "His name's Shaun."

"And …?"

"And … he was in a couple of my classes last year. We did that drama project together, remember, that one-act play? He's … nice."

"Come on, Vic. He's a teenage boy — he can't be that nice!"

"Mom!" Then people were really staring. I knew she was only teasing, but I didn't want to hear it.

"Okay," she said, "I'm sorry." Before settling right back into interrogation mode. "What does he look like? What kind of music does he listen to? Is he good enough for you?"

"Oh my god, shut up!" I so didn't feel like playing the best-friend game with her if she was going to keep being so annoying about it.

"Fine," she said, "keep it your treasured little secret. You're going to tell me. I know you want to."

We sat in silence for almost a full minute, which had to be some kind of record for us.

"You're really not going to tell me?" she asked when she'd finally drained her wineglass.

"No," I said, in the deadest tone I could manage.

Mom laughed.

"You never take me seriously!" I hissed. My voice was a hushed battle cry.

"I do take you seriously," she said, adopting an appropriately sombre tone.

"You don't," I said, rolling my head back. Okay, yes, I was being a tiny bit dramatic.

"I try to." She was being serious, so I stopped my moaning and sat still.

"Try harder," I said, my eyes shooting through her like a laser beam.

"I will."

And then she met my eye, giving me the same look that's charmed crowds across the country and all over the world. It's a little scary how powerful that look is, and that she can pull it out in a split second, shaking everything else off and making it feel like you're the only two people on the planet. I'd like to say that I'm immune to it, I should be by now. I know exactly what she's doing. But I know she means it too. She means it with everyone.

It sucks having to share your mom like that.

"I love you," she said, putting her hand over mine on the little plastic table.

"I love … schnitzel," I said, as our waiter appeared with two heaping plates of amazing-smelling food. Mom ordered a second glass of wine to go with her meal, while I checked out our waiter's toned arms through his paper-thin V-neck.

I was way too hungry to keep on hating her, so I focused my energy on tearing into my dinner instead. Mom was a bit better behaved with her chicken, and for once it was clear to the strangers around us which one of us was the adult.

When I'd shoved enough meat in my mouth that I finally needed a breather, I asked, "So what did John want?"

"Oh, we're speaking again?"

"I was hangry," I offered, in lieu of an apology.

"You were what?"

"Hungry plus angry equals hangry," I explained.

"Ha! That's great. Did you make that up, sweets?"

I shook my head. She gives me way too much credit; I'm not nearly that creative.

"No, Mom. It's just a thing people say."

"It's cute."

"Whatever. So?"

"Sooo …?" she said, dragging the word out like stringy cheese on a hot pizza.

"So," I asked, more pointedly, "why was John calling?"

"Oh," she said, "right. Well, I've got some shows booked."

"Oh, good." I got my second schnitzel-wind and started eating again. With my mouth full of breaded chicken, I asked, "Where are you playing?"

"Out of town," she said noncommittally.

She was playing with her food but not eating it, pushing her meat around the plate with her fork. She was stalling.

"How far out of town?" I asked, refusing to let her off easy.

"Oh, you know …"

"Obviously I don't." This was serious and she was still trying to shrug it off, so I persisted. "Where?"

She drained her second glass of wine. "Japan?"

"Jesus, Mom!" I tried to put my knife down, but accidentally threw it at my plate from the shock.

"And Europe."

"Whoa, that's … those're …" I fumbled with my cutlery, moving the knife off my plate, embarrassed at the noise I'd made. I lowered my voice, "That's huge."

"Yeah."

"Wow. That's like Dusty Moon big. Isn't it?"

"Yeah." She finally raised her head to look me in the eyes again.

"So how long're you gonna be gone for?" I asked.

"Sounds like it'll be two and a half weeks in Japan."

"Oh, okay," I said. "And Europe?"

"Six weeks."

It hit me like a punch in the gut. Eight and a half weeks without Mom. Eight and a half weeks with Gran. But I could see how guilty Mom felt about the whole thing already, so I played nice.

"Cool. Wow. That's, uh, that's a long time."

"I know, sweets, I'm sorry."

"So when is this all happening?"

"Japan in August."

"That's so soon! How can you even get ready in time?"

"I know, right? But they had some band cancel on them or something, apparently. There are a few folks touring together and I guess they had a spot to fill. I knew there was a chance it might come through, but I didn't want to get my hopes up. So now we've got three weeks to get ready!"

"Whoa. That's … you knew about this?"

"I mean, yeah," she said, "I knew the tour was happening, I just didn't think I'd get the spot. So I didn't want to get your hopes up. Or worry you. You know."

"Yeah," I said, "I guess that makes sense. But what about Europe?"

"Europe's news to me," she said, "but I've been wanting to get back there to play for a while now. I'll be gone September and October."

"Wow. Oh. Okay."

"Yeah," she said, "it's pretty wild stuff."

"But wait," I said, "when do you leave for Japan? When in August?"

"I'm not sure yet. We still have to firm up the dates."

"But it might be …?"

"I don't know," Mom said. "It might be over our birthdays."

Her hand was back over mine, but I shook it off.

"Oh?" I said. "Okay. Whatever. It's fine."

It only adds to the joke that Mom thinks of us as twins because our birthdays are so close together. I'm August fourteenth and she's August seventh. We're Leos, and we always celebrate our birthdays together. The parties are ridiculous, and they've gotten even rowdier as I've gotten old enough to enjoy them. Mom books a bar that one of her friends owns and it feels like everyone she's ever met comes out to wish her a happy birthday. And when they find out it's my birthday too, they go nuts. We wind up dancing 'til four in the morning and we're all just trying to hold each other up. It's amazing. Sticky and sweaty and perfect.

But Mom'll be in Japan this year, without me.

And I knew it would happen eventually, I guess, that we'd miss a year.

That our birthdays aren't actually worldwide holidays, even if it feels like they should be.

I knew it wasn't always going to stay the same.

But still.

# Three

So part of the reason why Mom's music is so popular is that people really used to love her old band. Like, obsessively.

People will just come up to us while we're out to talk to her. They want to shake her hand or high-five her, or ask her a million questions about a band that broke up more than ten years ago. Twelve, actually.

It happens all the time. A couple of weeks ago this young guy came up to Mom and me on the street. We were hauling flimsy plastic bags stuffed with actual groceries from an actual grocery store for once. Mom was even wearing a dress, though it didn't exactly fit her right, it was too loose in the chest — that was one thing I had over her: boobs. We looked almost like a normal suburban family that day, except for the fact that we were carrying our grocery bags on foot and not loading them into an SUV.

Anyway, as this guy walked toward us, Mom nudged me with her elbow and said, "He go to your school, hon?

Looks like someone's got a crush on you." Because his eyes were practically bugging out of his head staring at us, and for a second I almost thought Mom was right.

He was pretty cute. He was wearing these tight black jeans with beat-up Converse and a super-faded band T-shirt that you could practically see his ribs through. No way a skinny guy like that would ever go for me. Plus he was like half a foot shorter than I am, but Mom was right, it did look like he was staring at me.

He wasn't, of course.

When he got a bit closer you could see that he was trying to make up his mind about whether or not to say something. He was clenching and unclenching his hands and couldn't seem to look away from us, which was totally creepy.

"Are you … you're Micky Wayne, right?" he finally said as he approached us.

"Oh," said Mom, nodding, "yeah, that's me." She put down the two giant grocery bags she'd been struggling with and waved hello.

"Wow," he said, "wow. I'm such a huge Dusty Moon fan. Seriously. I even have a … can I show you my tattoo?"

"Sure." Then she turned to me as this kinda creepy but pretty cute stalker-boy started lifting up his pants leg to show us whatever dumb scrawl he had permanently marked on his leg. "You know you're not getting a tattoo until you're eighteen, right, Vic?"

"Uh-huh," I said, "just like you never gave yourself one when you were sixteen," I said, pointing to her left hand where she sported three tiny homemade tattoos

— *X*'s on the knuckles of her index and middle fingers, and a heart at the base of her thumb.

"I told you to drop it about the stick-and-pokes," she said. "Stick-and-pokes" being how a sixteen-year-old in Halifax is able to give herself a tattoo. And probably hepatitis. I Googled it — you dip a sewing needle wrapped in thread into some India ink, and off you go. Real sanitary.

"But I thought you were going to give me one for my birthday!" I said.

"Absolutely. I'm going to give you the Children's Aid logo so that they'll be able to recognize you when they come to take you away from me the next morning."

And by that time this weird kid had finally rolled up the leg of his too-tight pants and turned around to show us his tattoo of the Dusty Moon logo — the phases of the moon that Dennis, Mom's guitar player, drew for the cover of their first album — forever branded on the back of his left calf.

"Cool," Mom said. "Yeah, that looks great. I haven't seen one of those in a while."

He stood there, beaming at the attention, but made no attempt to roll his pants back down and be on his way.

"Look," Mom said finally when it was clear he wasn't taking the hint, "it was nice to meet you, but my daughter Vic and I really need to get our groceries home. All right?"

"Oh," he said, covering the tattoo back up, clearly disappointed, "yeah, totally. I'm sorry to bug you, it's just so great to meet you. Your music, it means a lot to me."

"I appreciate that," Mom said, giving him one of her smiles. "Take care." And we picked up our groceries and trudged the rest of the way home.

Not that it isn't cool to see people lose their minds like that over someone who I know deep down is a total weirdo and a slob, but it would be nice if once in a while the cute guys who stare at us on the street actually were looking at me.

Dusty Moon got their start when my mom was only just over a year older than I am now. She'd just turned eighteen when they had their first band practice. She was the singer, and her friend Dennis from school played guitar. Their bassist, Jason, and their drummer, Jana, were kids they'd met at parties, and they met up one day to see if maybe they could make some half-decent noise together. They hung out in Jana's parents' basement in Halifax, Nova Scotia, and together they banged out some tunes.

That was in 1996. Mom says that there was pretty well nothing happening that year. Musically, anyway. That Kurt Cobain had been dead for two years already, and that grunge music had become so mainstream that the corporate soul-suckage that all of those bands were railing against was, by that point, nothing but empty posturing.

So Mom, Dennis, Jason, and Jana started off playing stuff that sounded sort of grungy, but their sound started changing pretty quickly, and soon people started to take notice. They were recording a lot in Jana's basement with some really ancient audio equipment and somehow this cool label in the states heard their demos and signed them — I don't know how, this was basically pre-Internet — and then Dusty Moon started touring all around the world.

It's so unbelievable to me that she did all of that before she even turned twenty. There were shows that the band was booked to play where they weren't even allowed to hang out inside the club before they went on because they were too young to drink, which is hilarious.

When she was my age, Mom was off having adventures and giving herself tattoos, and pretty soon she was going to start a band that would make her famous and send her all around the world doing what she loved most.

And I spend my time trying to get one stupid drawing right.

I remember a few years ago when Mom was invited to play at some big music festival in Austin, Texas. There was a whole week of shows all over the city, with thousands of bands performing. Mom even took me out of school for a couple of days so that I could drive down with her and the rest of Dusty Moon. It was a reunion show, so it was kind of a big deal. Like I said, they used to be pretty popular.

The drive down to the fest was intense, but I got to sit shotgun in Bigfoot, Dusty Moon's old van. It's like a rule that you have to give your band's vehicle a name. I think it's good luck or something.

Anyway, Mom had just quit smoking for the seventeenth time, so she was pretty seriously grouchy. Jason and Jana were wedged in the back with all their gear and they all wanted to make the drive without stopping, so I pitched a fit when they wouldn't let me sit down at the fast-food place where we stopped for lunch. We all ate our burgers in the van instead, with me feeding French fries dipped in barbeque sauce to Mom as she drove.

It had been so long since I'd seen Jason and Jana that it was almost like a family reunion. They'd been like surrogate parents to me when I was little and on the road with the band, but on that trip we were definitely a dysfunctional family.

Everyone was in a bad mood. Jason's divorce had just been finalized and Jana had been fired from her new job as a server the day before we left because she'd asked for time off work. Mom insisted that this was illegal and made me promise I'd never take crap like that from a boss, which only pissed Jana off more.

Dusty Moon hadn't played together in years by then. And all four members hadn't even been in one place together since their last big show — the one where their guitarist, Dennis Mahler, announced that he was done with the whole thing, and that he didn't want to be in the band anymore. He said that the stress of touring, and recording, and trying to meet everyone's demands was too much, and he quit.

And they knew that Dusty Moon couldn't go on without him, but it was impossible for Mom and Jason and Jana to even imagine doing anything other than playing music. Dennis had been the heart of the band, but he had been acting so strangely in the year or so leading up to that night that they wondered if maybe they were better off without him. Maybe they could start a new band.

But then things got a whole lot worse.

I know a lot about Dennis, and a lot about what happened afterwards.

I know a lot about it because Dennis is my dad.

Or he was, anyway.

Or maybe he still is.

No. I don't mean that.

I know, I know that Dennis is gone.

That Dennis is dead and not coming back.

That Dennis is no one's dad, and never really was to begin with.

Dennis is — was just Dennis.

When Dennis was alive, he had icy blue eyes and shaggy reddish-blond hair. He loved the Beach Boys and Brian Wilson. He was tall, six and a half feet, which is why I'm so gigantic. He was never a surfer, but sometimes he'd pretend that he was. He'd talk about going down to Mexico to live with a bunch of yoga-loving gringos on the beach. Dennis had a dog named Charley, a mutt, who he'd named after John Steinbeck's dog. John Steinbeck was his favourite writer. Dennis played guitar, and he and Mom fell in love when they were teenagers. It happened fast. Dennis didn't finish school, he dropped out, but he was smart in other ways. He read a lot and kept a sketchbook, and he wrote most of Dusty Moon's lyrics himself.

Mom and Dennis were together off and on for a long time. They were dating even before they started Dusty

Moon, but they didn't always get along so well. But for whatever reason people absolutely loved their band, so they were stuck together for a long time, even though they knew that the two of them never really worked as a couple.

Dennis had some troubles. He had some difficulties, like, mental health-wise. Mom says that his troubles were just whispers in the beginning, but that they got louder and more demanding as time went on. He didn't always have both of his feet in the world that most people can see. I think that's what Mom liked so much about him. Dennis took his medications most of the time, but the pills stopped him from being himself, he said, so sometimes he wouldn't take them for a while and that's when things would get more intense.

And then, so the band bio goes, the night before they were supposed to head out on their first American tour, something pretty major happened. The band was going to drive through the States, playing as many shows as they could before they ran out of money, when my Mom found out that she was pregnant with me. She told Dennis that he was the dad and that she was going to keep me, and Dennis said that he'd do the best he could. They even gave me his last name at the hospital. They wouldn't let just Mom put her name on the birth certificate, so from day one I've been a Mahler.

They found out pretty soon after I was born, though, that it wasn't going to work between them. Dennis had too much of his own stuff to deal with before he could worry about anyone else. He got into drugs, too — heroin — on top of everything else, and Mom didn't want that stuff in my life. So they played together and they toured together, and they knew each other better than most people ever get to know another person — again, Mom's words — but she knew that he'd never be a good dad to me. And it was hard for her, I guess.

So anyway, after years of playing shows and recording and touring for months on end — Mom tried to bring me with her as much as she could, but she would leave me behind a lot, to stay with Gran and Grampa — Dennis finally announced that he was quitting. And nobody knew what to do. They knew that the band wouldn't be the same without him. So they went back to their crappy little hotel room that night and talked about what they were going to do next. Dennis wasn't there with them, they didn't know where he'd gone. They stayed up all night trying to figure out what to do, and eventually they decided that Dusty Moon would have to break up. Maybe, they said, they'd start a new band without Dennis.

Mom tried calling his apartment a few days later just to make sure that he was all right, but he didn't answer the phone.

Another week passed and she still hadn't heard from him. Nobody had.

And a week after that his parents took out an ad in the *Globe and Mail* that said DENNIS, PLEASE CALL US. WE MISS YOU. WE JUST WANT TO KNOW THAT YOU ARE SAFE. I know because Mom cut it out and saved it. It's in her Dennis album. The newsprint's yellowed and brittle now, but the message is still clear.

But he never called my mom or his parents or anyone. And they never found his body.

It's been more than ten years since it happened. But no one knows for sure what *it* was.

A few die-hard Dusty Moon fans still believe he's alive, which is so seriously freaky. The going theory is that he just packed up, changed his name, and left everything behind him. These fans, though, they're just desperate for an easy answer. They're like those people who still think Tupac's alive. That it's all some conspiracy. But we all know what really happened, and even Dennis's parents finally agreed that he was probably dead two years ago. They'd been holding out hope for a long time that he might come back, but I guess even they had their limits. They don't really talk to Mom and me anymore, but they send a Christmas card every year. Mom says she thinks it was just too hard for them to stay in touch, to see me. It's a pretty awful excuse, but I get that it's complicated. I think maybe Dennis's parents blamed Mom for what happened, but she doesn't like to talk about it.

They had to make it all official, though. To make him legally presumed dead. Mom got asked for a lot of interviews after that. The whole band did. They wouldn't talk about it, though. They said it wasn't respectful to Dennis.

Privately, Mom was glad that they'd finally done it. That they'd closed the book on him for good. She'd thought of Dennis as being dead a long time before that, and that's how she always talked about him to me. Dennis was a great musician. Dennis was so talented. Dennis loved your smile and your chubby little knees.

The Dennis I knew was always dead. That's all there is. I'm not some lost girl searching for the father she never knew. I'm not. I'm searching for a boyfriend, maybe, or sex on the beach. Or maybe just to find something I'm actually good at for once instead of hanging out in Mom's or Lucy's shadow while they do what they love.

So we ignore the message-board threads, blog posts, and conspiracy-theory Facebook groups. Dennis was a complicated guy, Mom says, so why shouldn't his legacy be complicated, too? She's full of all kinds of pseudo-philosophical nuggets of wisdom like that to deal with the weirdness of our lives. When she's not just plain full of it.

Some journalist is writing a book about it all. About Mom and Dusty Moon. And about Dennis. He's been trying to get Mom to talk to him for a while now, and she finally agreed to it after she read a bunch of his stuff and decided that if anyone was going to be able to tell the story respectfully it would be him. He's a talented writer, she says, even if he is a bit nosy. And Mom's never been what you'd call a private person. So she and Jason and Jana will finally tell the story of what happened to Dennis — or what they think happened, anyway — and some creepy journalist is going to make a bunch of money on a sad-sack story about my family. It feels like we're being used. Like this guy is stringing out our skeletons for everyone to see. There'll probably be a fresh wave of Dusty Moon conspiracy theorists, too. Thousands of people who'll think they know more about my family than I do just because they read some book. Great.

But anyway, the band and I were driving down to this festival in Chicago, this reunion show. I was twelve, I think, or maybe eleven. It was the first time Dusty Moon had played in years and their first time playing without Dennis. They figured he'd been gone long enough that they could sort of honour his memory by playing one last show together for a bunch of people who were dying to see them. They even donated the money they were being paid to a mental health centre in Toronto, which was cool, but also kind of stupid since Mom and I, and Jana and Jason, really could have used that money. Mom knew all of Dennis's guitar parts by heart, so she was going to play them and sing. They were excited to perform, I think, but they all knew how weird it was that they were reuniting without Dennis.

And I was so mad that everyone else was in such a bad mood on what was supposed to be my vacation that I snuck out to the pool of the motel where we were staying after Mom had gone to bed. Ignoring the sign that said WARNING: NO LIFEGUARD ON DUTY, I slipped into the deep end almost without making a sound. I flipped around underwater, then swam to the shallow end and practised my handstands. I splashed my head up and out of the water and looked up at the stars over our motel. There weren't many, but they seemed different from the ones at home. I counted them all, and then tried to do an underwater somersault for each one I saw. When I finally stopped, I was out of breath and my legs felt weak, but I didn't want to go up to bed. I wasn't done yet. I grabbed the towel I'd brought with me and dried myself off, then changed my mind and charged back toward the deep end, jumping with my knees up to my chest and yelling "Cannonball!" as loud as I could, not caring anymore if Mom or anyone else heard me. This was my vacation, too.

So of course Mom heard the noise and realized that I wasn't in bed like I was supposed to be. She came down to the pool in her robe and bare feet and instead of yelling and screaming like a normal mother would, she just sat down on one of the lounge chairs by the pool and gestured for me to sit next to her. I wrapped my towel around myself and stared at the water dripping off me on the concrete deck slowly forming a puddle.

"I'd really prefer it if you didn't sneak out," Mom said after more than a moment of silence.

"Uh-huh." I counted the drips as they fell, sometimes one at a time and sometimes in twos or threes.

"Just because we're not at Disney World doesn't mean that you can run off on me, you know."

"As if you'd ever take me to Disney World." Drip.

"Until they hire me to walk around in one of those giant suits, it's not very likely, no."

"You'd make a terrible Mickey Mouse." Drip, drip.

"Guess I'll have to stick with being Micky Wayne then, huh?"

"Haw haw." Drip, drip-drip, drip.

"So," she said, pulling her knees in to her chest, "did you have a good swim?"

"Uh huh." Drip, drip, drip.

"Good. Because the manager warned me when we checked in about E. coli in the pool. You might not be having so much fun tomorrow." Then she got up from the lounger and went back up to our room. I sat there for another minute before I followed her up, just staring at the surface of the water as the last ripples of my cannonball disappeared.

It was worth it, having my quiet, and then not so quiet, moment of rebellion. I was soaked in soggy satisfaction, and didn't care about tomorrow.

But of course she was right. I woke up the next morning feeling totally disgusting and sick because I guess I'd accidentally swallowed some of the water while I was swimming. And Mom took absolutely zero pity on me, so before I knew it she was practically throwing me in the back of the van with a barf bag in my lap, so that they could get to the main festival stage in time for their sound check. It wasn't long before the evidence of our continental breakfast made its way into that bag. Seven times.

So I spent the whole day throwing up into a bucket that some festival volunteer kept having to empty into a porta-potty for me. I barely even noticed where I was or who was playing. I felt like my limbs were made of rubber, and I couldn't have cared less when some annoying do-gooder tried to make me feel better by rustling my hair or generally treating me like a baby. But, rough as I was, Mom looked like her day was even worse.

She has all of these bad habits that come out when she's trying really hard to concentrate, like when she's writing a new song, or, in this case, when she was trying to kick nicotine. Again. She was biting her nails and scratching her scalp all day, and by the time it was their turn to play we both looked like we'd spent the whole day puking.

When Dusty Moon was finally up, the same volunteer who'd been dutifully emptying my barf bucket hauled me over to the stage, planting me behind the drums in a folding chair with my trusty bucket in my lap. I watched hundreds of people losing their minds over Mom, Jason, and Jana playing their old songs, singing along to every one and a few even shouting "I love you guys! Dusty Moon, yeah!" between songs. I don't know whether all of those people missed Dennis or not, but I'm willing to bet that they did. That they could tell it was different.

And in between all the love and adoration and everything else going on, I sat there, in what passed for backstage, watching all the tiny details of their performance. The way Mom went up on her tiptoes during her guitar solos, and Jana closed her eyes tight each time she hit her cymbals; the way Jason hung his head so low you could barely tell that he was grinning like a maniac the whole time, and the way each time a song ended there was this tiny flash of a moment when they all looked like they could barely believe that they'd pulled it off.

And I only puked once their whole set.

And, of course, a few dozen people took pictures of me doing it.

People are so gross.

# Four

A few days after the whole Hungary Thai double bombshell — I still couldn't believe that Shaun had texted me! — I woke up soaked in sweat from the city's heat wave that wouldn't even take a break at night. The noon sun nearly blinded me, even with my curtains pulled across the window. Okay, they're not exactly curtains — Mom and I hung a bedsheet on a piece of string nailed to the wall when we first moved in and we've never gotten around to replacing it. I was surprised that I didn't wake up earlier with Mom banging around the apartment while getting ready for work, but I was glad to have the place to myself.

Mom works a few days a week at a café/bar called Northeast Southwest that her friend Sal owns. Her shifts usually start pretty early in the morning to cater to the espresso-swilling, pastry-gobbling commuter crowd. Though sometimes she works late shifts, too, pouring pints of beer and mixing cocktails for twenty-somethings with waxed moustaches and too many scarves. She used to let me hang around while she tended the bar at night, waiting for her to be ready to go home, but one night I tried to sneak a beer while no one was looking and Sal got pissed. Like, super pissed. Mom said he was just stressed because they'd had a health inspection earlier that week that hadn't gone very well, but I still felt too embarrassed to go back.

I've asked her if she feels weird when people recognize her at work. Doesn't she feel ashamed to have people see her working at such a normal, boring job? She told me that it doesn't bother her, that she's just happy to help Sal out, and besides, record sales alone can't pay our bills. It works out pretty well though, since Sal's cool enough to let Mom blow off whole weekends at a time when she has to go out of town to play a show.

I wandered into the kitchen in my underwear and Mom's old Oilers T-shirt, and pulled our big skillet out of the cupboard to make myself a couple of fried eggs for breakfast, even though it was well past noon. I can never figure out the perfect moment to flip a fried egg over, so it always comes out a runny mess, but that's kind of how I like them. Or it's how I've learned to, anyway. I shook a ton of salt and pepper over top of the frying eggs, then slipped them out of the pan and onto a plate and squeezed a fat dollop of ketchup next to my slimy yellow breakfast. Mom may not be much of a cook, but she's taught me that there is nothing in the world more satisfying than a simple fried egg, messy or not.

I took my plate over to the couch and turned on a competitive cooking show that had just showed up on

Netflix. Mom and I don't have cable and she's paranoid about letting me download stuff, so I'm always a season or two behind everyone else. The show, called *Skewered!* — because I guess the world is running out of competitive cooking show names — was cool. I watched as a whole pack of tattooed chefs in white jackets tried to out-sauté each other, and I gulped down my breakfast, wondering how long each of the competitors had been training to get to this exact moment frozen in TV-time. I couldn't imagine how many hours they'd probably spent frying onions just to fight their way into this competition, derivative as it was. They were hot, too, almost all of them, though maybe that was just because they looked so confident. I imagined one of the burly bearded chefs making me breakfast — I bet they made amazing fried eggs. It was almost kind of depressing how talented they all were.

I turned the TV off and got up from the couch: green leather, inherited from Gran. My thighs stuck to the cushions in the heat and tearing them off the leather as I got up felt like someone had whacked the back of my legs with a canoe paddle. As if I've ever actually been canoeing. When the pain finally subsided, I picked up my plate and took it to the sink.

Then I went back into my room and picked my phone up off my night table.

No new messages.

I opened up my contacts and hovered my finger over Shaun's name, willing myself to text him, to type something, even something goofy or stupid. But then I thought against it, I didn't want to look desperate or like

I was trying too hard.

I put the phone back down and went into the bathroom to take a shower instead.

My face in the mirror was shiny from sweat and my hair was sticking out at strange angles from sleep. I rubbed the day-old mascara underneath my eyes off with my fingers, and then took off my shirt and started running a shower.

*I'll text him today*, I told myself.

It's fine, we made plans. He's expecting me to text him. It would be weird if I didn't, I thought as the water fell down on me.

Cold water, as icy as I could manage. It was the only thing I could think of to keep me sane in our oven of an apartment. The water pressure sucked, and Mom and I seriously needed to give the bathroom walls a scrub — everywhere you looked our long hairs were stuck to the ceramic tiles — but the shower definitely calmed me down.

*I'll do it*, I told myself.

*I'll text him.*

*I'll ask him to come to the beach with me.*

*It's no big deal. He already said yes.*

*I'll do it.*

*I'll do it today.*

*I will.*

When the water was finally so cold I couldn't stand it anymore, I shut it off and grabbed a towel. I tousled my hair and wrapped it around my head, not even bothering to grab anything else to cover up. Having the apartment to myself was the best feeling ever.

Back in my room, lying on my bed splayed out naked in a way I'm sure was really attractive, I grabbed my phone again.

"Just do it," I whispered out loud. And maybe the shower had numbed my nerves or something, but I texted Shaun: *Island trip?*

And, I swear, not thirty seconds later he answered, *You got it, V.*

I was thankful at least he'd left out the *Big* this time. And couldn't believe how quickly he'd answered. Still lying flat on my bed, I did a little happy-dance, waving my arms and legs like a wind-up toy. It was happening, just like I'd planned it, it really was!

*Cool*, I texted back. *Meet you at queen and brock in an hour?*

*Can't wait.*

I snatched my bikini — *the* bikini, the magic, perfectly fitting bikini — off the floor and put it on. I practically skipped back to the bathroom to admire myself in the mirror. The suit made even dorky me look awesome.

I struck a pose, or maybe twelve, to check myself out from every possible angle.

I turned my face a million different ways to figure out which side suited me best.

I pouted.

Then made a duck face.

I pulled my still-soggy hair into pigtails on either side of my head and stuck out my tongue at my reflection like a little kid.

I grabbed Mom's hairdryer and gave myself a once-over. The heat from the dryer made me sweat again, but no way was I going to meet Shaun with wet helmet-hair.

Because yes, I actually wear a bike helmet. Reluctantly. I've got a metallic pink skateboarder-style helmet that's pretty cool, but I'd love to get away with not wearing it. Fat chance, though. Mom has spies all over town, otherwise known as her near and dear friends, and I've been ratted out more than once when someone saw me flying down Queen Street with my hair flapping in the wind behind me. I sulked about it for a long time and refused to bike at all, but eventually I got over it. It was that or else retire my bike for good.

I tried on nine different shirts over top of my bathing suit, but wound up just sticking with Mom's Oilers shirt that I'd worn to bed. It smelled a bit funky from my sleep sweat, but it was vintage and kind of cool and sporty, which I figured Shaun would probably be into. He didn't have to know that I'd slept in it the night before, how would he? A pair of cutoffs completed the outfit, and then I went hunting through Mom's secret booze stash.

Contrary to the name, it's not really a secret. Mom and I just call it that because we think it's funny. Because we're above all that typical parent-kid hiding-the-good-stuff garbage. Mom keeps her booze on the top shelf of the pantry — a row of nearly finished liquor bottles of all different kinds. Mostly it's the stuff that people leave behind at parties for a reason, like flavoured whiskey, rice wine, and stuff that tastes like licorice. I pulled down a bottle of Captain Morgan that was a little fuller than the others and poured some of it into an empty water bottle from our recycling bin. I figured that if I left the house a bit early, I could grab a bottle of Coke from Lucy's parents' store to mix it with.

Mom wouldn't mind me taking just a little bit of rum, I figured. Besides, I was sure she'd done way worse things to Gran when she was young than scam a bit of booze. It was for a good cause.

Tossing my phone, keys, and the bottle of pilfered rum into my bag, I grabbed my helmet and headed down the stairs. Locking the door behind me, I whispered, "Things are happening!" and then laughed at myself for being such a dweeb.

Out on the street, I unlocked my bike: a cute but clunky red retro three-speed I call PYT (Pretty Young Thing). PYT's kind of heavy, so I don't usually bother carrying her up the stairs to our apartment the way Mom does with her fixie. She's nothing fancy, but PYT always gets me where I need to go. I walked her over to Lynn's Convenience where Lucy's mom (the Lynn the store is named after) was inside working the cash. I was smiling like an idiot as I paid for my Coke, and I noticed Lucy's mom looking at me funny.

"What are you up to, Victoria?" she asked.

"Oh, nowhere," I said. "I mean nothing. Just, uh, tell Lucy I said to say hi to her. Um, from me. Okay?"

Her eyes narrowed and I giggled nervously and then sprinted out of the store, waving goodbye, afraid that I looked suspicious. I heard Lynn yelling behind me that I hadn't taken my change, but it didn't matter; I couldn't be late meeting Shaun.

Outside I took a slug from my Coke and then hid in the doorway of a nearby shop that was closed down to pour the rum in. I turned the Coke bottle upside down a couple of times to mix it and then took a sip. It was good. Strong, but good. I took one more sip for courage.

I rode over to Queen and Brock — it wasn't far, just a couple of blocks away — and stopped to wait. I realized that I was trying to look in every direction at once not sure which way Shaun was coming from. *Be cool*, I told myself, *stay calm*. But it was way too late for that. The hummingbird in my chest was on high alert, and I could feel a bead of sweat roll its way from my forehead all the way down to my ankle.

Just when I thought that I couldn't stand waiting another second, I heard a voice from behind me and then felt a small tap on my shoulder.

"Hey," the voice said. "Hey."

I whipped my head around, nearly snapping my neck from the momentum. "Oh," I said, and then, forcing myself to be casual, "hey."

He was there. He really was. With sunglasses dipping toward the end of his freckled nose, and a smile that looked surprisingly shy. I wanted to just stand there and take him, and the moment, in, but it made me too nervous. I scoped out his bike, though, since it was far enough away from his face that I was able to force my heart to beat a normal rhythm. Shaun's ride was a royal blue department-store mountain bike, and it was definitely too small for him, with the seat raised up as high as it would go. It wasn't exactly what I'd pictured him riding.

"Oh yeah," Shaun said, laughing nervously. "It's my little brother's bike. Mine's in the shop."

"Oh," I said, "cool."

"Nah," Shaun said. "Not really. But, uh, should we go?"

"Yeah," I said, "sure. You wanna lead?"

"You do it," he said, "I'll follow you."

I smiled nervously and snapped my pink skateboard bucket to my head. He wasn't wearing a helmet. His hair was perfectly tousled and slightly spiked; I wanted to roll around in a whole field of it, maybe forever. I could feel my cheeks flushing again, so I turned away from him and mounted PYT.

"All right," I yelled over my shoulder. "Let's do this!"

"You got it," he called back to me.

With Shaun riding behind me I was so nervous I could've puked right there on the road. I booked it as fast as I could down the street, my legs straining to pound the pedals as hard as my body would let me. I turned around every so often to make sure that Shaun was keeping up with me, but he made my frantic pace look easy, even on his borrowed miniature bike. I pedalled harder.

We passed a giant park and a whole row of cute shops and restaurants that made up the trendy part of Queen Street West. Our neighbourhood was poorer, with more immigrant families and broke artists, though the trendiness had also started creeping our way with DIY bike shops and designer vintage clothing stores in between the roti shops and sketchy old-man bars.

I stood up on my pedals as we rode over a tiny hill that threatened to slow me down, and I gripped my brakes not a second too soon as a car parked on the side of the road chose the instant I was riding past to make a left-hand turn out of the parking space and back onto the road. I paused for an instant and then swerved around the car, just barely missing being laid out flat by a giant hunk of metal and machinery.

"Whoa, that was close!" Shaun called from behind me, as I tried my best to keep the pace. "You okay?"

I turned my head back to face him. "Fine!" I yelled.

I could feel the sweat from my forehead dripping down into my eyes and it stung.

"It's no problem," I said, looking back ahead of me at the road, "I just wish these cars would watch where they're going!"

"What?" Shaun yelled.

"I said I wish these cars would be careful of where they're going!"

"I can't hear you!"

"It's nothing," I said, giving up on being heard over the sound of traffic, and then, louder, "I'm fine!"

"Okay!" he yelled.

We managed to make it through a few construction snarls and down to the ferry docks in record time. We dismounted and started walking our bikes and I couldn't decide which would make me look stupider: wearing my bike helmet for the rest of the day, or revealing just how sweaty and disgusting my hair was underneath. Realizing that I'd have a pretty hard time justifying the former, I chose the latter.

"Wow," Shaun said. "You're really hot, eh?"

"Heh, yeah," I smiled nervously and turned away from him to fix my hair. "Gotta love this heat wave."

"Serious. I'm pretty sure I could fill an Olympic-sized swimming pool with my sweat. My parents' house is, like, an oven."

*Change the subject*, I told myself. *Change it quick or else you're going to be making dick and fart jokes with this mega babe the rest of the afternoon and he's only going to think of you as one of his dudes.*

"So," I said, pointing PYT toward the forming ferry line, "should we go and buy our tickets?"

"Oh. Yeah. I've never been to the Island before," Shaun said. "How does this, you know, work?"

"Seriously?" I said, at last feeling like I had the upper cool-hand, "My mom and I come here all the time. We buy our tickets over there." I said, pointing to the row of booths with giant lines of Island-goers in front of them.

"Ah, okay," Shaun said. "Cool."

We walked our bikes over and picked a line. When we finally got up to the front, I thought for a second that Shaun might offer to pay for my ticket, acting all chivalrous or whatever. He didn't, though. He bought his own ticket and then walked his bike over to the loading area just behind the row of booths.

Once I'd bought my ticket I had to dodge about a thousand sets of kids and parents to finally find him again, waiting with a small crowd by a gate marked HANLAN'S POINT ONLY: GATE #4.

"What's with the crowd?" Shaun asked, pointing to the gate next to us that was swarmed with families.

"That's Centre Island. There's a little amusement park there. It's got a log ride and stuff. My mom and I once went on it like fifteen times in a row."

"Oh yeah?" he said, taking off his sunglasses as we waited in the shade. "Cool."

"Yeah, the islands are all kind of connected but that one's, you know, for little kids."

"Sounds fun." He grinned, and I couldn't believe how huge his lips were. They looked, well, delicious.

"Oh, well, I mean, we could go," I said, suddenly losing any cool I'd picked up on the way in. "Do you want to? We could totally go to Centreville if you want. It could be fun."

"Ha, no," he said, waving me off, "it's cool, I was kidding. Wherever we're going is fine."

Of course. Could I not just play it cool for fifteen seconds?

The ferry arrived, and we walked with our bikes to take our place on deck. Everyone else on board looked older and more relaxed. They were snapping pictures with their phones and smiling and wearing cool hats and brightly coloured bathing suits under their clothes. And then the wind hit me and I finally got a whiff of myself. I was deeply, deeply funky. Why the hell did I leave the house in Mom's old shirt? I smelled disgusting. How was I going to manage this?

I tried at first to figure out exactly how strong the smell was — were other people around me stopping to look, or did no one else notice? What was Shaun doing, was he having a good time? Should we take a selfie together, just us, the ferry, and the waves? *No*, I thought, getting too close right now was definitely not an option. I was ripe.

"Wow, this is pretty great," Shaun said, his sunglasses back on, looking out at the sailboats nearby.

"Huh?" I said.

"I just meant ..." he said, turning to face me, "is everything okay?"

"Oh?" I said. "No. I'm not. I'm just. I'm so happy to be here, I can't believe you've never been here, the Island is the best! I love it so much!" The words tumbled out of my mouth clinging on to one another and I was helpless to stop them.

"Yeah," he said, looking me up and down skeptically. "I can tell."

"Oh," I said, reaching into my bag, "I almost forgot." I pulled out the Coke and handed him the bottle.

"Thanks," he said, "but I'm cool."

"No, seriously," I insisted, "you should try some."

He raised an eyebrow before taking a small sip. He smiled, and then took a gulp that drained nearly half the bottle.

"Nice," he said, handing it back with a wink. "Crafty."

I took a small swig and a trail of rum and Coke dribbled down my chin and onto my T. Perfect, just what the stank shirt needed. But I breathed in deeply through my nose and let the wind toss around my still sweaty hair. I could feel the tense muscles in my shoulders start to relax a bit. I just had to remember to breathe.

We docked a few minutes after that. We walked with the crowd getting off the ferry, and then as soon as I had the space to move, I hopped back on my bike. At least while we were riding we didn't have to talk. And I couldn't say anything stupid.

We rode more slowly than on the mainland. Shaun kept trying to catch up and ride beside me, but I fought to stay ahead, where he couldn't hear the words coming out of my dumb mouth. It only took a few minutes before we found the entrance to the beach. There was a little path that led to a boardwalk and we locked our bikes up nearby.

The sand was scorching hot on our feet and we walked in slow motion over the little hills of sand that finally gave way to the lake. It looked good enough to drink, though I knew that that was a terrible idea. Lake Ontario was a giant pool of poison, but it looked pretty good from the Island.

We inched our way closer to the water, and I pointed out a spot near a giant beach umbrella. "Is here okay?"

"Yeah," he said, "fine by me."

He took off his shirt and his sandals. His belly was soft and a little bit flabby, and his chest was pale and spotted all over with freckles. There were thousands of freckles, nearly blotting out the pale skin on his shoulders and his chest. I wanted to kiss every single one of them. Or his lips, at the very least. I dared myself to do it. I was buzzed already, but I definitely wasn't drunk enough for that kind of bravery.

I took off my shirt, grateful at last to have an excuse to stash the offending stench. *It's okay*, I told myself, *let the bikini work its magic. Just relax.* I rolled my head around on my neck in a full circle and felt a tiny crack. *Loosen up*, I thought. *Loose. Loose. Loose.*

I laid my towel out and flopped down onto it. I breathed deeply and tried to slow my heart to the speed of the crashing waves. "More?" I asked, offering him the spiked Coke.

"Sure," he said, stretching out on the sand next to me.

But as I reached over to pass Shaun the bottle, my eye got stuck on something.

Something yellow.

Fluorescent yellow.

A huge, hairy man in a tiny fluorescent yellow bathing suit.

The huge man turned around — it was a thong!

"What?" Shaun said, noticing my wide eyes. "Oh, yeah, I guess this is, like, a nude beach, huh?"

"What do you mean?" I asked, turning to look behind me as my eyes bugged out of my skull like a chihuahua.

Naked people. Men, mostly. Old ones. Wrinkly ones with beef-jerky skin. There were some young people, too, though. A group of girls with their tops off were playing a game of volleyball not far from where we'd sat down. Their boobs jiggling as they jumped up to hit the ball.

Naked people.

A beach full of them.

That was where I'd taken Shaun on our first date — a naked beach.

Did he think I'd brought him here on purpose? That I wanted to take off all my clothes in public — or worse, that I wanted him to? He'd think I was some kind of pervert.

I could see naked people everywhere now. There was so much skin. How had I not noticed as we sat down?

I felt sick, nauseous. I was going to hurl. I was going to puke in front of all the naked people on the beach. Oh god, they were so, so naked. They were everywhere.

A couple in their seventies walked past us on their way across the sand and offered a wink and what I'm sure they thought was a friendly, knowing nod.

Oh god.

I had to go.

"I've gotta ..." I said, grabbing my putrid shirt back out of my bag and pulling it back over my head. Somehow the smell was magnified now, like it had been put under some kind of smell-microscope.

"What?" Shaun said, polishing off the bottle of Coke.

"Go," I said. "I need to go home. There are some things I need to ..." I grabbed my sandals and shoved them back on my feet. "I'll see you ... are you? You're ...?" I couldn't pick a sentence. All the nakedness had short-circuited my brain.

"Huh?" Shaun said. "You're leaving?"

"You're, uh, staying?" I asked. I smelled like sewage, worse than sewage. What smells worse than sewage?

"Yeah," he said, shrugging, "guess I will."

"Okay, cool," I said. "I've just — I've got to go."

And I ran away as fast as the sand would let me.

I ran like a dumb little kid.

I unlocked PYT and wouldn't let myself cry. I wouldn't. Though I could feel hot tears of embarrassment stinging the backs of my eyes, I held them in.

I pedalled back to the ferry, nearly letting the tears go with gratitude when I saw a boat waiting for me. I took my place on the deck, faced out where no one could see me, and I let the hot tears spill down my face. People around me nudged each other — asked, "Do you smell that?" but I just kept on silently sobbing.

Once we were back on the mainland, I couldn't get away from the ferry docks fast enough. I cut up Bay Street to Queen, and rode even faster than I had on the way over, trying to outrace my shame as sweat trickled down my forehead, stinging my eyes. I felt painfully sober.

I finally stopped at a red light at Spadina Avenue — my breath was ragged, and I was nearly out of air — but the second I saw the other side change from green, I stomped back down on my pedal, flinging my body into the intersection.

I couldn't stop riding.

I didn't ever want to stop.

It was unbelievable. Unbelievably humiliating.

Cars skidded around me and blared their horns as I flew through the lights — it was an advance green, I realized, and cars were trying to turn left around me, but it was too late to stop, I had to keep going. My chest was tight with panic as I realized the mistake I'd made, but I finally relaxed enough to breathe as PYT and I cleared the intersection. I closed my eyes in relief — just for a split second, an instant, I swear.

And that's when I got doored.

# Five

At least seventeen different people told me how lucky I was that I'd been wearing my helmet when it happened. It wasn't a ton of consolation, though, while I lay there on the sidewalk feeling like my arm had been snapped in half, that my idiot brain hadn't been goo-ified along with it. Someone had the sense to pull PYT off the road, but she'd been totally mangled in the collision and seeing her lying on the sidewalk with all the wrong angles sticking out hurt almost as bad as my arm did.

What kind of loser rides through a red light at a major intersection without a single freaking scratch, only to get doored on the very next block?

The woman who doored me — the woman who flung open her driver-side door without looking for any particularly distraught-looking cyclists on the road, sending me flying off of my bike and onto the asphalt — was in hysterical tears when the cops showed up. Someone walking by must have called 911 after it happened, because the police cars got there quick. When they arrived, though, they spent nearly as much time consoling the woman who'd almost killed me as they did making sure I was okay. But I was way too out of it with pain and humiliation to protest.

She tried to apologize to me — the hysterically crying, carelessly dooring woman — but every time she looked at me she just lost it, and I couldn't make out any of her squeaky, terrified words even if I'd wanted to.

The ambulance arrived on the scene pretty quickly, too, but I almost died for real when I saw a cute paramedic with dark, floppy hair and cool retro glasses open the side door and make his way toward me.

Oh, come on! They couldn't have sent a hunchbacked medic? Or one with an uncanny resemblance to Steve Buscemi? Oh no, no no no, send out your cutest indie-rock-geek guy to mop up the putrid mess of me, please. Say, handsome, did you know that I'm none other than the only child of former Dusty Moon songstress, Micky Wayne? Why, of course I can get her to sign your ID badge for you! She'll be so thrilled that the man here to care for her daughter is a fan — she might even take you out to dinner!

"Are you all right? How's your pain?" Medic Fanboy asked, snapping me back to reality as he checked me out — fortunately, considering how thoroughly disgusting I was in that moment, it was only in a medical sense.

"It hurts. My arm," I said, trying my best to keep my arms down at my sides so that this gorgeous guy couldn't get a whiff of my blood-, Coke-, and tear-stained stink-bomb of a shirt.

But it was useless, and I finally had to give in to my total mortification as a team of professionals fussed over me, got me up on a stretcher, and loaded me into the ambulance. I closed my eyes and started counting by threes, hoping to somehow lose myself — my mortification, my throbbing pain, and my utter and complete stank — in the numbers. It was an old trick Mom used to use when I was learning my times tables to keep me distracted while she practised.

3, 6, 9, 12, 15, 18, 21, 24 …

But it didn't work.

It was a short ride to the hospital and somewhere in my delirium I must have told someone to call Mom at Northeast Southwest, so it wasn't long before she found me, spaced out and trying to trick myself into believing that this whole nightmare of a day had been just that — an awful dream.

I could smell Mom — a combination of espresso, maple syrup, and lavender — even before she swooped in on me with a truly classic expression of parental concern: "Jesus Christ, Vic, what the hell happened?"

Somebody get this woman a Mother of the Year trophy, stat.

"Hi, Mom," I mumbled, half-nodding toward an elderly couple sitting nearby us who seemed a bit taken aback by the volume of her concern, which was turned up to eleven. "It's fine," I said, nearly chewing off my tongue as it wagged lazily around my mouth. Whatever they'd given me for the pain seemed to have seriously taken control of me. It was kind of nice. A welcome distraction from my garbage dump of a day.

"What the hell happened?" Mom repeated at an only slightly lower volume. Clearly she hadn't taken the hint.

"I was stupid, okay?" I said, waving her off. "I was stupid. I did a stupid thing. A stupid, stupid, stupid —"

She grabbed me by the chin and made me meet her eyes. "What. Happened."

I fidgeted until I could get my chin free, and then explained, "I got doored."

"By a car?"

"No," I said, already exhausted from her line of questioning, "by a pegasus."

"On your bike?" she insisted, taking my chin in her hand again.

"Yes," I said, meeting her eyes with a dull stare.

"But the car that hit you —"

"I got doored, okay?" I said, shrugging my shoulders to the best of my limited ability. "I'm just a big idiot. A big, dumb idiot, okay?"

"Oh, sweets," she said, "that's not your fault — it was the driver who was being careless."

"It wasn't exactly —" I started to say.

"Thank God you were wearing your helmet!"

Eighteen.

"Mom, it was … like, sort of my fault. Kind of. I wasn't really — I mean, I wasn't paying that much attention. I was kind of … I was upset, okay?" I lowered my voice to a pain med-slurred whisper. "Just sad. I was really sad."

"You were so sad you biked into a car?" she said loudly enough so that everyone, including the cute medic who was filling out paperwork nearby, could hear.

"Shut up," I hissed. My arm was still dully throbbing and I'd reached a boiling point. "I finally got up the nerve to text Shaun today, okay? So we went out. And it was horrible and embarrassing, and I left but he didn't, and I was biking home and I rode through a red, which was stupid, which I know, but I was fine, and then this car …"

And then Mom wrapped her arms around me. Tight. Which was actually kind of a dumb thing to do since I couldn't really move my right arm because it hurt so badly; she was probably making my bones warp. So we sat there — technically I lay there, since I was still on the stretcher — with her arms wrapped around my middle, my left arm sticking out like a scarecrow and my right arm, in a sling, squeezed hard against my torso. Classic Mick and Vic.

And in that moment I hated her, but there was no one else in the world I wanted to see.

They took me in for X-rays and showed me what bones I'd broken: my wrist and my thumb.

"How long is it going to be like this for? How long will I have a cast?" I asked the emerg doctor with the cloud of ginger hair who seemed to be in charge of me. I couldn't stop staring at his orangey halo and I'm pretty sure he could tell. He pretended he couldn't, though. What a pro.

"It'll be six to eight weeks, I'm afraid," he told Mom and me grimly. "Hope you weren't planning on writing a novel this summer."

I refused to dignify his terrible joke with a laugh, though Mom gave a small dad-joke chuckle for his benefit. I would've grouchily crossed my arms if I'd been physically able to manage it, but my injured arm stole the gravity of my favourite protest pose.

Six to eight weeks without my right hand and thumb meant I wouldn't be playing *Lore of Ages V* any time soon — or finishing my portrait of Stara. Lucy could probably play the game one-handed, but I was so slow to begin with, and so not a lefty, that I knew I wouldn't be able to manage with my cast on. And drawing was most definitely out. If my skills had been weak before, I was straight back to kindergarten now — pass the crayons. The icing on the whole crap cake was that there was no way I'd be back on PYT any time soon. Even if she hadn't been mangled in the accident, the idea of getting back in the saddle made me way too nervous.

*Great*, I thought. Not only had I ruined my chances with Shaun forever and was never going to be in with Lucy's hardcore *LoA* friends, but Mom was going to be off to Japan any minute, and I couldn't even ride around town on my bike to stave off being bored to death without her. My eyes started leaking in a way that I swear on Stara Shah's leather jacket was against my will.

Doctor Ginger Cloud gave us directions to another room down the hall where I'd have my cast put on and then he left the two of us alone. Mom turned to me and then noticed my involuntary eye-slobber.

"Aw, sweets, don't cry," she said. "It's okay, that's not such a long time to have the cast on. It'll be off before you know it. It'll be off by the end of the summer — the fest! And in the meantime, I'm going to sign it, I LOVE MY DAUGHTER VERY, VERY MUCH AND SHE'S THE SMARTEST AND PRETTIEST GIRL IN THE WHOLE WORLD, EVEN IF HER CYCLING HABITS LEAVE JUST THE TEENSIEST BIT TO BE DESIRED."

"Mom," I said, weakly laughing through my dumb tears, "seriously, shut up."

"Do you think they'll let you pick your cast colour? Like DayGlo green, or camou or something?" she said, getting up from her chair. "Come on, let's go, I want one, too!"

"Stop it," I said, pointing my weak left hand at her to sit back down. "Would you just — can you, like, listen to me for a second?"

She sat back down next to me on the examining table, kicking her sneakered feet. "What's up?"

"I don't want you to go to Japan," said my drugged-up mouth, to the great surprise of my brain. I mean, sure, it was what I'd been thinking, but I didn't have any intention of telling Mom that.

"Oh, honey," she said, giving me her charity-smile like she knew I was stoned out of my gourd. And, I mean, I was, of course, but that smile still totally pissed me off.

"Seriously," I whined. "Why is it so important? It's-it's … stupid. What's so good about Japan?"

"Sushi, for one," Mom said, retracting her pity.

I couldn't believe that after all I'd been through that day that she still wasn't taking me seriously. That she couldn't just for one second be a normal mother.

"You're the worst," I whine-yelled like some spoiled

four-year-old who'd been told they couldn't eat candy before dinner.

"Ohhh-kay," she said, reassessing the situation and getting up off the table to stand in front of me. "What's really bugging you?"

"It's you!" I said, giving in and letting my drug-induced neediness take total control. "You just — you just leave. You keep leaving. You leave me here. With Gran. And I hate it, I'm sick of it. It's stupid."

"Yeah," Mom said, unmoved, "you mentioned that."

"And you never listen to me when I'm upset!"

"Well what do you want me to do?"

"I want you to stay," I said in my smallest voice ever. I couldn't look her in the eyes, so instead I studied the intricacies of the hospital floor.

"But you know that I can't, right?" Mom said, her voice almost as small as mine.

"You could quit." I was pushing it, I knew. This wasn't going to end well, but I wasn't sure I wanted it to.

"And do what exactly?" Mom asked. "Work at Sal's place every day?"

"You could get a real job."

I was going for blood. Or my tongue was, anyway. I couldn't stop it. It was flapping of its own free will.

"This is my real job," Mom said, for once using a serious parental tone. "Lots of people travel for work. I mean, I know it sucks sometimes — and believe me, it sucks for me, too, this isn't just about you. It gets lonely on the road. And it gets boring and — but, anyway, it's what I love. It's who I am."

"For now," I said. The venom kept coming.

"Look," she said, "I'm sorry if you don't always like it, but this is who I am, all right? Your mama's a wandering wind."

"Oh good," I said, speaking slowly to make the sure the arrows of my words stuck hard in her chest, "you're writing song lyrics while waiting for your daughter to get a cast put on her shattered arm."

"Let's talk about this later, okay?" Mom said, suddenly looking as exhausted as I felt. "The doctor's waiting for us. And I don't think they were exactly planning for a monster family brawl in emerg tonight." She was pulling mom-rank. And sober-rank. All I wanted was to be able to cross my arms.

"Fine," I said. "Let's go."

"Come on, Eeyore," she insisted. "Time to hit the casting couch."

I wouldn't even meet her eyes, I knew they'd be wide with delight at her own terrible joke and I couldn't believe that she was still trying to be my best friend.

"Worst. Joke. Ever."

They put the cast on — plain white, despite Mom's insistence that I choose something more interesting — and told me not to get it wet.

"It's just like in *Gremlins*," Mom said excitedly on our cab ride home, trying to keep things upbeat despite our unresolved argument.

"I don't know what you're talking about," I said. I didn't want to offer her anything that could be construed as curiosity.

"Oh, come on," she said, reaching to slap my arm before remembering that it was now wrapped up in a plain vanilla cast. "You know. That movie? They were these, like, cute, fuzzy little critter-guys, but if you got them wet or fed them after midnight or — I forget, there was some third rule — they'd turn into gremlins. And they terrorized the city!"

"I still have no idea what you're talking about," I said.

"I think you might need a few more T3s to get yourself prepared," she said, jabbing the little pharmacy bag of painkillers that lay between us on the car's back seat.

"The drugs for my broken freaking arm are not to be used to help you conjure some dumb movie that doesn't even exist," I said, trying to sound as snooty and offended as I could, which was tough because I was so completely zonked and also I was still pretty stoned.

"The dope fairy has a lot of rules, huh?"

"What does that even mean?" I said. "Are we going to finish what we started talking about back in the hospital, like, ever?"

"We will, sweets," she said, "of course. But I think you've had enough for the night. Let's just watch a movie and sort this stuff out later." She'd totally read my mind, but I wasn't willing to give up the fight just yet.

"You do know that this isn't how normal parents act, right?" I said.

"No one in the history of the world has ever accused me of being a normal parent."

"Obviously." I exhaled audibly and tried my best to let it go, just for the night. "And anyway, you're totally making this movie up. *Gremlins* is not a thing. And it's definitely not on Netflix."

"That's it? You're finished with your attack on my child-rearing capabilities?"

"Rearing?" I asked. "Since when have you reared anything?" But I stopped myself from going any further. Plus the word *rear* was sounding really weird in my mouth. "Look, I'm exhausted, okay?" And I was. There were so many more things I wanted to say to her, even yell at her. But right then all I wanted to do was crawl into her bed and watch a movie on the laptop we share custody of. "I'll make it up to you tomorrow."

"I'll bet." She put her hand over mine on the back seat of the cab and held it there for almost a whole minute without speaking.

"But I can't believe I never showed you *Gremlins*! It's the best. The best. It was basically my all-time favourite movie growing up."

"So it was a stone age blockbuster? I hear their DVD players sucked."

"The ice age, actually. Their Blu-rays were surprisingly advanced."

"Oh yeah, chiselled out of snow and permafrost, right?"

"Exactly. And *Gremlins* was the best of the icy best. Hmm, you're sure it's not on Netflix?" She raised her voice then, and called to the driver, "Excuse me, slight change of plans. Can you drop us off at 7-24 Video, please?" The worst-named place in town, which was also our regular. "It's right at Fuller, just up here."

Yes, my mom and I are probably the last people in the world who still rent movies. Blame it on Mom's downloadophobia. Like that's the most surprising thing about us?

I crawled out of the backseat, hauling my smashed arm behind me, while Mom paid the driver.

I wanted so badly to believe that we could just have a normal movie night and pretend that nothing had happened, and that we had nothing more to talk about and could just go back to being ourselves. But I could tell that things were bubbling up just below the surface. I wanted my perfectly-normal-to-us life. For nothing to change, even though I sometimes hated Mom for being the weirdo she was. But it was already happening, I could tell.

# Six

Mom and I stayed up until almost two in the morning watching *Gremlins*, which, as it turned out was a thing. It was pretty good. The parts of it that I saw, anyway. I passed out, drooling on Mom's shoulder for the last hour of the movie, jolting awake just as the credits started to roll.

We were slow getting out of bed the next morning.

"You mind making breakfast?" Mom called as she finished doing her makeup in the bathroom.

"You do remember that I broke my arm, right?"

"Aw, come on," she said. "You can still fry up a couple of eggs, can't you? Please? I'm so late."

"What," I asked, getting the carton of eggs out of the fridge, "did you finally get sick of the muffins at work?"

"Are you kidding?" Mom said. "Francisco's muffins are the best in the state!" Francisco is Sal's boyfriend, practically his husband, and does all the baking for Northeast Southwest.

"Canada, Mom," I said as I took the skillet out of the cupboard. "We live in Canada."

"I know," she said. "But best in the province doesn't have nearly the same ring to it."

She had a point. "Okay," I called, "so why no muffins, then?"

"I've just been starving lately, I go through four or five muffins during a shift and Sal's not such a fan of me scarfing down his profits."

"At least someone has business sense," I said, clumsily cracking an egg with my left hand. Half a dozen fragments of shell landed in the skillet along with it. These eggs would definitely be Mom's. "Besides, how can you be so hungry with this heat?"

"Dunno," she said, coming out of the bathroom, with her hair still half-wet and hanging around her shoulders, but with flawless eyeliner — somehow on her that combination looked good. "Maybe I'm pregnant again."

"Not funny," I said, trying my best to flip her sloppy eggs. "You've got to finish with one daughter before you start on number two."

"But don't you see?" she said, coming up behind me to give me a weird half-hug. "I could fix all the screw-ups I made with you. I could have a perfect kid!"

She was joking. I knew she was joking. But the fact that we still hadn't resolved our conversation from the night before and she was feeding me lines like this, ones she knew would irk me, got me pissed. While Mom crossed the apartment to change, I turned up the heat on the stove and watched her eggs slowly sizzle and burn.

"Geez, Vic," she said a couple of minutes later when she'd finally finished getting ready. "It stinks in here."

I scooped her scorched eggs out of the skillet and onto one of the plates I'd set out. Putting down the serving spoon, I handed them to her. I was amazed at how long it took to do anything with only one good arm. "Breakfast."

"Huh," she said, surveying the slop. "Guess I better work on my material, eh?"

"It's better than you deserve," I said, half under my breath.

"Ouch. Hey, be nice. Remember who your human slobber rag was last night."

"You're the worst," I said, turning the heat back down on the stove so I could cook my own breakfast.

"Hey, Vic, look at me." She put down her plate and, taking me by the shoulders, made me turn to face her.

"Ow, god, Mom, my arm, remember?" I struggled out of her grip and massaged my right shoulder like I was in serious pain, even though it didn't actually hurt. If Mom was going to be as annoying with all of this stuff as she was, I was going to play up the arm as much as I could.

"Oh right, yikes, sorry!" she said, trying to pet my arm like a dog, as if that was going to help. "But, look, can we talk about this?"

"What, now?" I said. "You're on your way to work."

"Okay, fine, then when I get home?"

"You're sure Sal isn't going to ask you to work a double again?"

"I'll tell him no," Mom said. "You and me, okay? Tonight."

"Fine."

"Great," she said, picking up her plate again and dumping the burnt mess into the garbage. "But I told you, I don't like my eggs flambéd."

I knew it was stupid and wasteful, but still felt smug satisfaction as I ate my own eggs, which were a little sloppier than usual but still delicious, and definitely not burned. I cleaned my plate and then checked the time. Ten-thirty. What was I supposed to do with myself all day?

I pulled out my phone and texted Lucy. It took me ten minutes just to type my message out. Apparently the fingers of my left hand were a lot rustier than I thought.

*You have to come over*, I texted. *I broke my arm.*

*What?* Lucy answered, *How?*

*Just come over. Please?*

*K*, Lucy texted, *be there soon.*

It was almost two hours before Lucy got there. I went back to bed for an hour and then screwed around on the computer for a bit, checking Instagram and looking up random stuff on Wikipedia, including a page that looked like a twelve-year-old girl had been using it as her diary. Weird.

Everything was harder with just my left hand, and turning the doorknob and opening the door when Lucy finally rang the bell was a surprisingly difficult job.

"What took you so long?" I asked, as I let Lucy in.

"Oh stop it," Lucy said, racing up the stairs to our apartment, "this is worth the wait, trust me."

"What," I said, "did you bring me a new arm from your parents' store?"

"Oh yeah," she said, pausing to get a good look at my cast. "That looks bad. What happened?"

"Ugh. Long story," I said, grateful for some sympathy from someone who wasn't about to take off on tour without me. "Sit down, you want a popsicle?"

"Sure," Lucy said. "Purple me."

"Clearly."

I clumsily grabbed two ice pops out of the freezer and dropped them on the coffee table in front of the couch.

"Can you open mine for me?" I asked, pointing to the pink one.

"Wow," she said, "you really can't do anything now, can you?"

"Let's just say that *LoA* is on hold."

"Yeah," she said, "I figured." She gestured to my arm. "So?"

"I got doored," I said. "On my bike. I was riding home from the Island. I was on a — you know, I was hanging out with Shaun."

"Oh?" she said, sucking thoughtfully on her popsicle. "I thought you said he was an idiot."

"You said he was an idiot. I like him."

"Why?" she asked. Hadn't we been through this before?

"'Cause he's cool and cute and, you know …"

"What?" she bit the rest of her popsicle and pulled the sticks out of her mouth. My teeth hurt just watching her.

"I like him, okay? I really like him. But I totally screwed up. It was so embarrassing." I hugged my knees to my chest with my one good arm and waited for Lucy to ask me how the date had gone so badly, but it was clear that she had something else on her mind entirely.

"Yeah," she said, "that sucks. But, look, I've got to show you what I found."

"What is it?" I asked, as Lucy opened up the laptop on the coffee table. "A new *LoA* trailer or something?"

"Just wait," she said. "Jazleen was posting about this last night. She's so jealous 'cause she lives in Peterborough and they don't have one."

"One what?" I asked. Jazleen is one of Lucy's best online friends, and she's going to be visiting Toronto at the end of the month just to go to Fan Con. She's really cool but kind of intimidating. I follow her Tumblr and am constantly amazed that she seems to know more about what's going on in our city than I do.

"Just wait. This is going to blow your mind."

Lucy typed a few short words into the search bar and then turned the computer around to face me.

"She Shoots?" I asked, reading the first search result.

"Keep reading," Lucy said, perched over my shoulder like an oversized parrot.

I clicked the link and read the banner at the top of the page: SHE SHOOTS — SUPPORTING GALS IN GAMES SINCE 2012.

"What is this?" I asked, confused, but somehow already excited.

Lucy's face was basically broken, she was smiling so hard, and she started talking a mile a minute as she caught me up on what was clearly her new favourite thing.

"Look, it's this group, right?" she said. "And they help you make your own games. It's amazing!"

It did sound kind of amazing, but I still had no idea what exactly Lucy was talking about. "How?" I asked.

"They hold these game jams, see?" Lucy said, pointing to an event listing on the screen. "Where you make a whole game over a weekend. They're doing a jam next month all about food, so all these people are going to get together and make games about, like, eating and stuff. Isn't that cool?"

I'd never seen her this excited, which was really saying something, because *LoA* made her practically rabid.

"And, like, anyone can join?" I asked.

"That's the best part," Lucy said, "it's just girls. Or, you know, women. At least, some of the events are."

"Wow," I said. "Cool."

"They're even tabling at Fan Con!"

"Great," I said, "something else I'll be missing out on."

"Oh right, sorry," Lucy said distractedly. She was still poring over the site, like she was trying to drink in the coolness of the group through her eyeballs.

"So, like … should we join?" I asked.

I wasn't even sure if this was the kind of group where I'd fit in, but, I figured, it might at least help my case with the *LoA*ers. Besides, it was something to do, which meant that it met all of my basic requirements. And with Mom on her way out of the country and any more action with Shaun now officially impossible, it seemed like pretty much the only choice.

"That's kind of the problem," Lucy said, finally pulling herself away from the screen. "I don't know if they'd let, like, kids join."

"We're sixteen!" I said.

"I'm fifteen," Lucy reminded me. "And anyway, I don't want to show up not having any idea what's going on. I want them to think we're …"

"What," I said, "cool?"

"Experienced," Lucy corrected me. "I don't want to look like some poser, you know?"

"Oh, come on. Nobody would ever accuse you of being a fake geek girl," I said. "Your *LoA* obsession alone speaks for itself."

"Yeah," Lucy said, "but I don't know any of the systems they're using."

"So?" I said. "Isn't this whole group about, like, teaching you that kind of stuff?"

"Look," Lucy said, ignoring my reasoning, "they have a tutorial up on their website. It'll show us how to make a basic text-based game. You remember that game *Zork* I showed you a couple of months ago?"

I remembered sitting in front of Lucy's computer at her house, watching her type commands into a text-prompt that told us we were standing in front of a house. She told me that it was one of the first-ever computer games. Which was cool, but I had trouble picturing the scene the game was describing without any graphics, and we kept getting eaten by something called a Grue.

"Yeah," I said. "Why? Can we make something like that?"

"Totally," Lucy said. "And it can be about whatever we want."

"Wow," I said, "that sounds cool. But isn't it, like, hard?"

"Not really," Lucy said, taking over the computer again to find another site. "There's this software called Twine that we can download for free. Then you just write your scenes and map them all out together. I already tried it at my place. It's great."

"Except we can't download it. You know how my mom is."

"Like she'd even notice."

"No, seriously," I said, "when she found out we'd down-loaded those old system emulators last year she totally flipped out. She gave me this whole lecture about how we'd opened the gates of hell to a bunch of viruses or whatever."

"Your mom's weird," Lucy said. "That's her biggest concern?"

"She's a total technophobe. I'm just glad she hasn't started hassling me about sexting."

"Yet," said Lucy.

"Whatever," I said, scanning the page that she'd pulled up, "look, there's an in-browser version anyway. Let's just use that."

After a two-second tutorial on how to save our work, Lucy and were looking at a perfectly blank page.

We decided to write a tiny game, just as a test, so we put together a seven-screen story called *No, Seriously, I Really Love Lucy* about Lucy finding a unicorn hidden behind the chip rack at her parents' store and going on an incredibly short adventure. The first screen introduced the story and then gave you two different links to click on to decide what happened next; would Lucy try to speak to the unicorn or call magical pest control instead? Depending on which option you chose, you'd get a different screen with more story and another two choices until you finally reached THE END. The best ending saw Lucy and the unicorn flying off into space for more adventures, and the worst one had her eaten by a family-size bag of Cool Ranch Doritos. The game was super goofy, but it was pretty fun to make. And Lucy was right, it was easy. Between the two of us we could really make something cool.

We test-played it four times so that we got all the different endings, but then Lucy checked her phone and said she had to get going.

"Come over tomorrow," she said, "and we'll start plotting out our real game."

"You're sure you can't stay for dinner?" I asked, mentally counting the hours until Mom was due home from work.

"Sorry," she said, "I've gotta go."

"All right," I said, "I'll see you tomorrow."

"Cool," she said. "G-Day."

"Huh?"

"Oh, you know," she said, smiling self-consciously. "Game Day."

I nodded and we high-fived before I closed the door behind her. It was going to be great.

But tomorrow felt like forever away.

I wanted to keep on messing around with Twine, but the blank page was too intimidating on my own. I was itching to build another story and see how far I could take it, but I didn't know what story to tell. I needed Lucy for her big ideas.

Without even thinking about it, I wound up in a YouTube hole, and soon enough I was looking up clips of old Dusty Moon shows. They always seem to show up in my recommended sidebar, but maybe that's because I can't help clicking on them whenever they show up.

I've watched most of them already, but that day there was a new video I hadn't seen before. It was just a bunch of footage that some fan had put together of a few of the bands' shows. I hit play and lay down on my side on the couch with the screen tilted at an angle so I could see it. My bulging, sweaty thighs stuck to the couch and each other and the tiny jean shorts I had on were helpless to stop them.

It was weird and kind of comforting to watch the band play, but it was nothing I hadn't seen before. The songs I've heard over and over again: "Stranded in Daylight", "Shadow Tree," and "Fixing to Fix You." The same chords and the same melodies. I'd heard them so many times they were almost white noise to me now. That is until the live footage abruptly stopped and a scrolling text screen, that looked like a six-year-old kid had picked the font, appeared in its place.

DENNIS MAHLER, 1978–2005

MISSING, PRESUMED DEAD

...

OR IS HE???

*Oh god*, I thought, *another conspiracy theorist whack-job. Great.* But I looked at the date that the video had been uploaded. It was only a week old and it already had ten thousand views.

REPORTS THAT DENNIS HAS BEEN SPOTTED IN HUATULCO, MEXICO HAVE BEEN CONFIRMED BY INDEPENDENT SOURCES

DENNIS MAHLER

...

...

...

IS ALIVE!!!

Jesus. They really couldn't leave it alone, could they? And why did anyone else think this was their story to tell?

Like this journalist, the one who was writing the book, whoever he was, was sucking blood from Mom's and Dennis's story. He was a leech, trying to profit off some supposed Canadian alt-rock mystery. And he was probably creaming his pants over this latest fake news. Oh, sure, Dennis was in Mexico the whole time. Why didn't anyone think to look for him there?

There was no mystery.

There is no mystery.

Dennis is dead, and anyone who says otherwise should get their tinfoil hat examined. They all just need to get a life.

I lay there for hours, watching every Dusty Moon clip I could find on YouTube. As repulsed as I was by this new video and the horrible grave-digging rumours that were going to come with it, I couldn't stop watching the old concert clips and music videos. It was like I was in a trance.

When it was almost dark, I finally realized that I could feel a cloud of perspiration on my shirt where my cast had been pressed against my stomach all afternoon. I needed a drink, a cold one. And more painkillers.

It took me nearly twenty minutes just to get the dumb cap off the bottle of pills in the bathroom. The childproof top was nearly cast-proof too, as it turned out. I tried every conceivable combination of pressing my cast down on the lid while turning the bottle with my left hand, but it kept falling out of my grip and onto the floor — still blanketed with Mom's hair since she rushed out of the apartment in such a hurry that morning. When I did finally manage to pop the top off, I was so unbelievably frustrated that I dumped two pills onto the counter and swallowed them with a big gulp of water from the tap. One pill, I knew, was all I really needed, but I figured that if it was going to take a million years just to get the pills open each time I needed one that I might as well make it worth my while.

A few minutes later, I started to notice the lightness in my limbs, and that my head felt like a helium balloon full of stones. Smooth, smooth stones that slowly knocked against each other any time I moved my head. I giggled to myself. I was totally high.

On the other side of the room, my phone started vibrating. The harsh whir it made shaking against our cheapo IKEA coffee table made me jump, but I managed to answer it after half a dozen rings.

"Hey, sweets."

It was Mom, of course. I hoped she couldn't hear that I was stoned.

"Hello," she said, "you there?"

I realized that I'd been so paranoid that I hadn't actually opened my mouth yet.

"Yeah, hey. Hey," I said, trying to make my voice as steady as possible. In my head it sounded too deep and way too slow.

"Hey," she said, clearly not noticing the difference. "Look, I can't really talk right now. I just wanted to let you know that Sal asked me to work a double and, well, there's no one else who can cover the shift and we're totally swamped. It looks like I'm going to be closing. I'm really sorry I'm not going to be home for dinner like I promised, but we'll talk tomorrow, all right?"

More silence on my end. She was talking too fast and her voice sounded like a high-pitched whistle.

"Come on," she said, "you're not mad at me, are you? There's nothing I can do about this. I can't leave Sal here by himself. I can't."

There was nothing to say. It was just one more time she couldn't keep her word. One more time that she told me I couldn't be upset that she'd totally broken her promise. One more time when she couldn't just step up and be a freaking mom.

"Vic?" she said, now anxious that I wasn't responding. "Are you there? I'm going to be home late, yeah?"

Was everything a question now?

"Yeah, yeah, whatever," I said, catching my breath. My chest felt like it was being squeezed tight like a stress-ball. "See you later."

"Okay," she said, "I've gotta go. And I'm sorry again, okay? But don't wait up, I'll be home late. I love you!"

"Bye."

I took the phone from my ear and put it down on the counter. A part of me couldn't believe that she'd gone and broken her word — again, again, again — but the stoned part of me, which, by then, was most of me, couldn't believe I was going to get away with being totally wasted.

I poured myself a tall glass of water — no ice, of course, Mom hadn't thought to make any — turned off the computer and pulled up an old Disney movie on Netflix instead. I laughed my face off at scenes I'd watched a hundred times when I was a kid, and clapped my hands with glee at the end when the beastly dude turned into a regulation hunk. I drained a couple of glasses of water, but then I started craving something sweet. I looked for juice in the fridge, but we were all out. It was seriously sad how Old Mother Hubbard our kitchen was. There was only a tub of wilted baby spinach along with two bottles of mustard, a box of baking soda, and a half-empty bottle of white wine.

I took the wine out of the fridge and put the bottle down on the counter in front of me. It was a big one, the size of two normal wine bottles, because Mom said it was cheaper to buy them that way. Then I got myself a small glass from the cupboard. It was a cup, really. A souvenir from the time Mom's old boyfriend Fletcher took us to Medieval Times. Even half empty, the bottle was still too heavy for me to lift with my left hand, so I wound up spilling about as much wine as I managed to get into my cup. I shuffled across the small puddle on the floor in my sock feet to clean it up, giggling to myself at the idea that my foot was going to get drunk from the wine. Which made me giggle out loud at how dumb my brain was on painkillers. When I'd mopped up most of the puddle, I peeled the winey socks off my feet and tossed them in the direction of my bedroom.

"Bottoms up!" I said to myself as I slurped from my cup of wine.

I looked at the cup more closely, twisting it around to see the cheap hologram effect of the plastic. "I don't believe I'm supposed to be drinking, Lord Windermere," I said, addressing the galloping knight on my plastic chalice.

"We shan't let your mother know," I replied in a fake-deep knight voice. "Besides, most surestly it is her own fault for leaving her one-armed daughter alone with nary a crumb in ye olde refrigerator. And besides, shouldn't she be home by now … eth?"

I giggled and downed the rest of the cup, then poured myself a bit more. My head was feeling impossibly heavy, like a boulder tied to a kindergarten-craft pipe cleaner. I fumbled my way toward the couch. My feet were heavy now, too, and my stomach was rocking dangerously back and forth. I put Lord Windermere on the floor beside me and curled up to take a nap.

I woke up when I heard a key in the door. Mom was finally home. I picked up my phone from the coffee table and saw that it was three in the morning. My eyes still felt tacky from sleep and I could barely keep my eyelids open.

"Aw, sweets, you really shouldn't have waited up for me," she said in her quietest voice as she opened the door. "How you feelin'?"

Putting her purse down by the door and kicking off her sneakers, she moved my legs and sat down next to me on the couch.

"How was your day?" I asked groggily, half sitting up to look at her.

"Oh, it was fine, just long," she said, stroking my leg. It was hypnotizing, and I almost fell right back asleep when Mom spoke again.

"Vic, what's that?" she asked, pointing at Lord Windermere.

"It's nothing," I said, reaching out to grab my drinking buddy.

But Mom's reflexes were a lot faster than mine and she beat me to it. She sniffed it. "Is this my wine?"

"Just a little bit."

"I don't care how much you had," Mom said. "Do you have any idea how stupid it is to drink while you're on painkillers? Jesus, Vic, you could have killed yourself!"

"It's not exactly like there was anything else around to drink," I said, my mouth dry like a wrung-out sponge. "I was thirsty. I only had a tiny bit."

"I can't believe this. I can't believe you'd do something so stupid. Did you even think about what might happen if you mixed them?"

"Well maybe if you hadn't left me alone all day!" I countered, pushing myself up to a full sitting position. My head was still heavy, and I weaved forward and stuck out my hand to keep myself up.

"No, you are not turning this around on me," she said. "I had to work, okay? Like an adult. This is about you." She shook her head. "God, I can't believe this, Vic. I don't even know what to say right now. Just go to bed." She wouldn't even look me in the eye.

"Whatever," I said, slowly getting up, my hand still braced on the couch. "Maybe if you were a real mother."

She looked like she was about to cry, but she didn't. Her breath got caught in her throat for a second, but she swallowed it back down before she spoke.

"I'm sorry, okay?" she said. "I'm sorry I let you down. But you scared the hell out of me, you have to understand that."

"Yeah," I said, my shame slowly building, "I know, no more mixing."

"I'm serious, Vic. You have to be careful."

"I know," I said. The tears running down my face were involuntary, prescription drug-induced, I was sure. "I will."

"You promise me," she whispered in my ear as she pulled me into a death-grip hug.

"Ow, Mom," I said, mid-hiccup, "my arm, remember?"

"Oh. Sorry. Just go to bed, okay? I have the day off tomorrow. I'm all yours."

"Okay," I said, extricating myself from her. I wandered off to my room as she dumped the rest of Lord Windermere down the drain, shaking her head.

"I'm going to kill you," she called.

"I wouldn't recommend it," I said. "That's child abuse."

# Seven

I slept in late the next morning, and when I finally woke up it felt like there was a mountain of sand on my chest, weighing me down, and I could barely get myself out of bed.

"The beast stirs," Mom said, coming in with a mug of coffee and putting it down by my bed. "Thought you could use some caffeine."

I picked it up and took a small sip. "This stuff tastes like paint thinner."

"Oh, so you've been drinking that, too?" she said. "We really have a lot to talk about."

"Would you grab my T3s from the bathroom?" I asked, putting on my most pathetic face. "Please?"

"One," she said, offering up a cautionary finger and wagging it in the air. "I'm getting you one pill."

"Thanks, Mom," I said, taking another sip of coffee and grimacing.

She came back to my room with the pill and a glass of water in her hands, and I swallowed it gratefully before laying back down on my bed. Mom sat next to me and ran her fingers through my hair. "So," she said.

"So?"

"Do you want to start, hon?"

"I told you I was sorry about last night," I said, brushing her hand away from my head.

"I'm not so sure you did," she said.

"Well I meant to."

"So …?"

"So?"

"Go ahead." She pushed my nose like it was an apology button.

"I'm sorry, okay? I'm sorry I drank your wine."

"And the pills?" she asked.

"Mom, I need those pills. My arm hurts so bad."

"I know you think you need them," she said, "just take it easy, all right? And don't ever mix like that again. You could have killed yourself."

"I thought you were the one who was going to kill me."

"I still might," she said, "I haven't made up my mind yet."

"Hello, 911?"

"Har har. So. Now that we have that settled …"

"That's settled?" I asked. "Wow. I got off easy."

"You have no idea."

"Some. So, are we done here? My head seriously hurts." I stooped to take another sip of coffee and hoped that the Tylenol would kick in soon.

"Surprise, surprise," she said. "But before I leave you to wallow in your hangover, I thought maybe we could talk a little bit about the tour."

"What's there to talk about?" I asked.

"Well, maybe I'm reaching here, but I'm going to go ahead and use my stunning psychic abilities to guess that maybe there's something about the tour that's bugging you."

"Well, yeah," I said. "It sucks that you're gonna be gone for so long, but I know it's important to you, so whatever. It doesn't matter. Go."

"It won't be that long, sweets," Mom said. "You'll barely even notice I'm not here. We can video-chat all the time!"

"Yeah, uh-huh," I said. "I know."

"Is this about our birthdays?"

"Come on," I said, "I'm not some dorky six-year-old. I can handle us not being together for our birthdays."

"So what then?" she asked.

"What do you mean *what*?"

"Why is this bothering you so much?"

Mercifully, the Tylenol was starting to kick in, and I could feel my whole body start to relax. My tongue loosened, slip-and-sliding around in my mouth, and I heard myself say, "Because you didn't even ask me to come with you."

Immediately embarrassed at how childish I sounded, I curled up onto my side, facing the wall. But Mom lay down on her side next to me and hugged me close with one arm around me, like we were spoons in a drawer. "I wish you could," she said quietly into my ear. "I really do. But it's almost two thousand dollars to fly to Tokyo and back again, and we just don't have that kind of money right now."

"Oh," I said, mad at myself for not having considered the cost of the trip in all my disappointment.

"I'm working as much as I can for Sal just so I can afford my own ticket. I'm really sorry, sweets. I wish you could come. I'd love it if you could. But I'm pretty sure the only way we could afford it is if we bought two one-way tickets."

"Look out, Tokyo," I said to the wall, "here we come."

"You think they'd let us move into one of those cat cafés?" Mom said, sitting up.

"What are you talking about?" I said, turning to face her.

"Come on, Vic, you've heard of them, haven't you? They're these places where they charge you by the hour and you get to hang out with a whole bunch of cats!"

"Wow," I said, "heaven really is a place on earth, huh?"

"It'll be great. We'll eat sushi and soba all day, and we can get matching koi-fish tattoos!"

"Mom, seriously, where did you learn about Japan, *Sailor Moon*?"

"Wikipedia," she said proudly.

"No wonder you're so wise."

"Of course. So wise that I'm willing to take my chances on your temporary good mood and tell you that I think you should give this Shaun guy another chance."

"Yeah. Right."

"I'm serious, hon. It can't have been that bad. Besides, you're going to need to work up some juicy gossip for our video-chat dates while I'm away."

"You're terrible," I said. "This is my life!"

"And you owe it to yourself to give it a decent shot. What's the worst that could happen?"

"You mean other than accidentally taking him to a beach full of naked old men for our first date?"

She sat up and leaned back on her hands. "How full of naked old men are we talking exactly?"

"Full-full," I said, sitting up, too. "Neon thongs and beef-jerky skin as far as the eye could see."

"Ha! Oh god, that's hilarious. You should be writing this stuff down, it's a great story. Ooh, or a film, a short little movie!"

"Mom!" I smacked her leg. "This is real! Not some stupid punchline for your next burst of inspiration."

"Have it your way," she said. "But real life always makes the best stories." She picked up my coffee mug from the floor. "You want any more of this?"

I shuddered. "Ugh, no. Thanks."

"Suit yourself," she said, and was about to leave when she turned back and said, "I really do think you should give that boy another chance. You could use someone to keep you company. Besides Lucy, I mean. And your gran."

"You could use someone to keep you quiet."

I went over to Lucy's house later that day so we could start plotting out our game. Lucy comes over to our place more often than I go over to hers because she says she likes how quiet our apartment is — when Mom's not around, anyway — but I love Lucy's because it's the exact opposite, always busy, and that day was no exception. Lucy's dad was fussing around in the kitchen cooking something that smelled delicious, while her aunt kept watch on a giant pot on the stove and two of her little cousins tore through the place, pretending to be Batman and Bane.

"Come on," Lucy said, shutting the door behind us to her parents' small home office, "this is the only place my cousins won't come looking for us."

She moved some stuff off of the big desk on the far side of the room, turned on the computer and opened up Twine, which she'd downloaded, to start our new game fresh from the beginning.

"Shouldn't we make some notes or something first?" I asked.

"That just means typing stuff out twice," Lucy said. "Let's just do it."

"Okay," I said, less than convinced that trying to write a game together without a plan in mind was such a great idea.

Lucy started off by writing the scene for our opening page, and she told me to look away as she started typing frantically. Obviously she'd had an idea in mind already. I distracted myself by looking at the piles of papers and framed family pictures hung on the wall until finally Lucy told me that she was finished.

"What do you think?" she said, leaning over me to reread her words while I looked at them for the first time on the screen.

I'd only read a few lines of what Lucy had written before I started to get a weird feeling in my stomach.

It was about a young woman time-traveller who found herself transported to an ancient Mayan village.

"Cool," I said, trying to be as positive as I could. "This is sort of like an *LoA* tribute, right?"

"Yeah, I guess, kind of. But it's just a starting point. I mean, we could go anywhere with this — the story's wide open."

"I just meant …" Was I wandering into a friendship bear-trap? It didn't feel like there was any good way out of this. "Maybe we should do something more original?"

"I don't only write fanfiction, you know," Lucy snapped.

Definitely a bear-trap.

"I know, I know. Look, I'm sorry, okay?" I said, trying to back-pedal. "I was just hoping that our game could be, you know, more personal. I mean, I thought the whole point of making our own game was to tell our own story."

"Fine," Lucy said, "go tell your own story, then."

"What?" I said. "We only just got started. Let's just keep going and see what happens. I like this as a start, I think that there's lots we can do with it."

"Sure," Lucy said, "we can copy *Lore of Ages IV*, scene by scene. Because that's all you think I can do, right?"

"That's not what I said!" I was getting mad now at how indignant Lucy was. She was just pissed that she'd been so obvious. That wasn't my fault.

"Whatever," Lucy said, turning back to the screen and deleting what she'd written to start over again.

I could feel anger tightening like a fist inside my head, and I was about to leave without saying another word when I remembered that I had absolutely no other plans for the rest of the summer. That Mom was about to leave. And getting another chance with Shaun definitely wasn't going to happen. She Shoots sounded absolutely amazing, but there was no way I could go on my own. I didn't think I'd done anything wrong, but I was just going to have to apologize anyway.

I sighed and sat back down next to her. "I'm sorry, okay? I was a jerk. I'm sorry."

Lucy wouldn't even look up from the screen, which was still blank. "You were."

"I know," I said. "Forgive me anyway?"

"Yeah," Lucy said. "I guess so."

"Come on," I said, "let's grab, like, some paper and a pen and sketch out some ideas."

"Fine," Lucy said, grabbing a pen and a small spiral-bound notebook from the drawer of her parents' desk and sitting down cross-legged on the floor. "You're so retro"

"Blame my mom," I said, taking a seat next to her, "she's got me, like, stuck in the nineties."

We spent the rest of the afternoon brainstorming until we finally came up with an idea that both of us liked. We decided to make a game about a creepy old house, where you could explore different rooms that led from one to another. We couldn't decide on what the ending would be, or even a name for the game, but figured that coming up with descriptions for each of the rooms and what was in them would give us lots to work on before we had to figure out what the point of it all was.

After that, I started going over to Lucy's house almost every day so we could build our creepy mansion together, room by room, and it was amazing how quickly the next few weeks passed. Lucy and I were in our own little world, texting each other with new ideas for the game when we weren't together working on it, and I was so glad we'd found a way to work together without killing each other. She was the only friend I had who hadn't left town for the summer.

I didn't mention the game at all to Mom. Not because she wouldn't have wanted to hear about it, but because I liked it being Lucy's and my secret project. Mom had a bad habit of trying to horn in on my extracurricular activities, and she was still hurting from the time I refused to start a family band with her. Never mind that my lack of musical talent or ability to carry a tune made the idea a total impossibility.

I told her about the new Dennis video, though. And by the time I actually got around to showing it to her, the video was up to almost eighteen thousand views.

"Wow," she said, as the text of the video started scrolling, "people really believe in this stuff, don't they?"

"Eighteen thousand of them," I said.

"Huh," Mom said, "I always thought that if he was going to go anywhere, Mexico would be the place."

"Yeah?" I said.

"Oh yeah. Open up a gringo bar on the beach and go surfing every day. He would have loved that."

"I thought you said he didn't surf."

"Oh, no," Mom said, "he didn't. He was actually kind of afraid of the water. Still, it's a nice thought. He would've adopted about a dozen street dogs by now."

"Do you miss him?" I asked.

"It's hard to say. But I feel him with me. I do. Every day."

And then it was time for Mom to leave. She and her band had been rehearsing overtime to make sure they were in their best possible shape for the road, and most nights she didn't get home until long after I'd fallen asleep.

"You know what I hear Beyoncé does before she goes on tour?" Mom asked as she packed up the last of her suitcase. Of course she'd left it until the last minute — she was leaving the next day.

"What?" I said. "Luxuriates in the aura of being powerful and perfect?"

"Of course," Mom said. "But seriously, I hear she runs on a treadmill while singing her entire album front to back. In heels."

"So that's why you've been spending so much time at the gym," I said, an obvious joke. Mom had never set foot in a gym in her life. She was one of those people who are annoyingly skinny no matter what they eat.

She'd definitely been gone more than usual lately, though, which was kind of weird. She'd chalked it up to working extra shifts for Sal and practices running late, but there were nights she'd come home looking more like she'd been fooling around in some asshat's shoebox of a condo than wiping up strangers' spilled beer, and I was starting to get suspicious. This was nothing new, of course. Mom went through boyfriends at a surprising rate considering she had such a mouthy dependant, but she's never made me meet them unless it was serious, and for that I was glad, glad, glad.

"You know me," Mom said, "I've got them buns of steel." She stuck her butt out at me, shook it and laughed.

"A regular Jillian Michaels over here," I said. "When's your TV show air?"

"Any day now. We'll blow those Biggest Losers out of the water with my new program: *Fork Yourself Fit.*"

"Uh-huh," I said, sitting down on Mom's suitcase to help her zip it shut. It was overloaded with more clothes than she'd possibly need in Japan along with half a dozen books because apparently she was too punk rock for an e-reader.

"Thanks, sweets," she said, inching the zipper around the suitcase. "Now stay with me here. Raise your fork to your mouth and chew. Good, that's one! And down to your plate — excellent! Now back up. That's two! Keep going!"

"Great plan," I said, "I'll start working on a Fit Fork app."

"Ooh, that's even better. Almost … aha! Done!" She did a little victory dance at having finally forced her bag closed.

"So, what time are we meeting Gran at the restaurant?" I asked as I helped Mom lift her suitcase up onto its wheels.

"Oh geez, seven at Queen Pasta," she said, checking her wrist for a watch that wasn't there. "What time is it now?"

"Uh, six forty-five?" I said, pulling out my phone. "But it's close by, it's right on Queen, isn't it?"

"No," she said, "it's one of those stupid suburban tricks. It's all the way out in Bloor West Village." Mom was exaggerating. Gran's neighbourhood wasn't actually the suburbs, but it was far enough west of where we lived that it brought out the downtown snob in her. Which was weird considering that we hadn't even lived in Toronto that long.

"So what now?" I asked. "That'll take us at least half an hour. And Gran'll be pissed if we're late."

"I don't know," Mom said, sounding like a nervous little kid. Gran definitely brought that out in her.

"Jam jar?" I asked, nudging the small Mason jar sitting on our bookshelf where Mom kept her emergency money. She'd even made up a dorky label for it that said THE OUT-OF-A-JAM JAR.

"I guess we don't have a choice, huh?" she said. Mom was seriously stingy about dipping into the jar, especially since we'd already taken one cab ride that week, but the thought of facing Gran's wrath was enough to foil her cheapskate ways. This time, anyway.

"Not unless you've invented some way to teleport since yesterday."

"I was so close," Mom said, "did I tell you?"

"Uh-huh," I said, grabbing my phone and jabbing her with my elbow to point her toward the door. "So what happened?"

"I think I forgot to carry the one."

"Har har. Come on, Gran's probably already there."

She locked the door behind us. "Do we have to?"

"Are you willing to let me stay here by myself while you're away?" I asked, walking down the stairs.

"And come home to you passed out on pills, struggling to open a jar of peanut butter? Not likely."

Mom spotted a cab coming down Queen toward us and flagged it down.

"When are they going to make that stuff in a squeeze bottle, anyway?" I asked, opening the backseat door.

"Maybe we can use that million-dollar idea to pay for the next cab ride. But in the meantime," she said, climbing in and shutting the door behind her, "we better roll."

Despite the jam-jar cab ride we were still ten minutes late meeting Gran. She was already at our table with a glass of white wine in hand and a magazine opened in front of her.

"Hi, Gran," I said, coming around to give her a hug.

"Just a minute," she said, pointing to the article she was reading and brushing away my arm without looking up.

She stopped when her hand collided with my cast and finally looked up from her reading — some sciencey thing, from the glimpse I got of a multicolour brain scan. "What happened, Michelle?"

Naturally she asked Mom and not me. Naturally she used her full name, which no one but her ever does.

"It's nothing, Mom. Vic was just in a little accident on her bike. Tell her, honey," Mom said, accidentally jabbing me in the arm.

"Ow," I whined, rubbing my cast.

"Oops, sorry, sweets. Let's just sit down."

The restaurant was a lot fancier than the places Mom and I usually ate, and I felt self-conscious as I sat down and tried to tuck the chair back under the table by scootching my butt forward. It scraped loudly across the floor and the couple at the table next to ours both looked up from their fettuccine to gawk at me.

"Are you all right, Victoria?" Gran asked.

"I'm fine," I said, as much to her as to the nosy couple next to us.

"I don't like you riding your bike downtown," Gran said. "It's dangerous. I'm surprised it's taken this long for you to get hurt."

"Really," I said, "I'm fine."

I waited for Mom, the certified cycling nut of the family, to come to my aid before realizing that she was staring intently at a waiter across the room, attempting to lure him over to our table to bring her a glass of wine.

But I wouldn't let her off that easily. "Mom bikes almost every day and she's never been in an accident."

"Oh really? I seem to remember you winding up in a cast much like this one when you were Victoria's age," Gran said to Mom. It was like I didn't even exist for her except as a weapon to use against Mom. I couldn't believe I was going to have to stay with her while Mom was running wild all over Japan.

"Let's just drop it, okay?" Mom said as the waiter brought her psychically summoned wine to the table. "Vic's going to be off her bike for the rest of the summer, anyway, so you won't have to worry about it while she's staying with you."

"Fine," Gran said, clearly making an effort to bite her tongue and avoid a scene. "Shall we order?"

The meal dragged on, punctuated by four pieces of bread and butter, on top of the heaping plate of spaghetti carbonara I ordered for dinner. I figured that if I at least kept my mouth full I could avoid having to answer Gran's mind-numbing questions about what courses I'd be taking at school next year and try to jam the pleasure centre of my brain with carbs to trick it into thinking we were having fun.

Gran kept going on and on about this article she was reading. The one we so rudely interrupted her from when we showed up for dinner. It was something about brain chemistry and genetics, but I could barely follow her train of thought. Mom was just smiling and nodding and getting the waiter to refill her wine glass as often as she could manage.

We sorted out the details of Mom's flight and when she would drop me off at Gran's house and got the bill just as my bread binge started creeping up on me and I felt so full that I thought I might explode. Mom and Gran bickered over the cheque until Mom finally grabbed the little plastic folder with our bill in it and made a break for our waiter on the other side of the room.

"Your mother always has to make a scene," Gran said less than quietly.

"She just wanted to do something nice before her big trip," I said, holding my stomach with my good hand to try to stop myself from feeling nauseous.

"She should be holding on to the money she has."

Mom came back a minute later wearing her exhausted triumph like a feathered cap. "Let's boogie."

Outside the restaurant we said good night to Gran. I went to give her a hug, but she said, "I'll see you both tomorrow. There's no need for a big goodbye now." So we put her in a cab home and started walking toward the subway.

"My stomach hurts," I moaned, when Gran was finally out of earshot.

"My head hurts," Mom said, taking my cast in her hands. "Let's go home."

The heat wave finally broke that night and there was almost a chill in the air from the breeze coming off the lake. We piled into our apartment and collapsed onto each other on the couch. I reached out to grab the remote from the coffee table, but Mom stopped me.

"Just wait a sec," she said. "There's something ... well, there's something I've been meaning to tell you."

"We're getting a pony?" I asked.

"Oh yeah, he can sleep in the bathroom and run wild through the expanse of our tiny apartment."

"We'll call him Captain Buttersworth," I said, giving a small salute.

"Yup, a real noble gentleman. But seriously, Vic. This is, well, I just want to tell you something."

"Okay," I said. "So no pony then?"

"Better luck next life, kiddo. This is about the trip. You remember that journalist? The one who's working on the book?"

The book. The Dusty Moon book. My mom and dad's unofficial biography.

"Right," I said. "What was his name again?"

"It's Ken. Ken Yoshida. He's, well, he's actually going to be coming with me. With the band, I mean. But he's coming to interview me."

"Why?" I asked. "Like he can't just interview you here?"

"I've been so busy, you know? We've hardly had time to sit down and he has a lot of questions for me. You wouldn't believe the research he's done. I think he probably knows more about me than I do."

"So he's paying two thousand dollars to hang out with you in Japan? That's creepy, Mom. That's super creepy."

"It's really not that big a deal, sweets. Ken was planning a trip to Japan to visit some family anyway, and it just happened to be around the same time as my tour."

"That's a pretty big coincidence," I said, unimpressed. "You're sure he's not, like, stalking you or something?"

"I don't think I've quite reached the level of fame where I have to worry about stalkers, sweetie. I'm not Tiffany."

"Who?"

"You don't know Tiffany? 'I Think We're Alone Now'?"

"Not ringing any bells."

I knew I had a choice. I could go for the throat and make Mom tell me why she was being so weird, why she'd waited until the last minute to tell me that this creep Ken was going with her to Japan. I could start a fight that would last until she left the next morning and make us both furious, while she flew halfway around the world to do exactly what she wanted to do. Be Micky Wayne the rock star.

Or, I could keep my mouth shut and enjoy my last night together with my de facto best friend.

I seriously needed better friends.

So instead I turned on the TV and we watched a double-bill of *Empire Records* and *Say Anything* and I passed out, drooling, in her lap.

# Eight

Way too early the next morning, Mom shook me awake.

"It's time," she whispered.

I offered her a primordial grunt in response and Mom left me alone to finish waking up. I packed up the last of my stuff into my giant backpack while Mom hauled her pile of luggage to the front door.

"You're not going to do anything stupid while I'm away, are you?" she asked.

"I should ask you the same thing."

"And you'll be nice to Gran?"

I let out a jumbo-sized yawn. "Uh-huh."

"And you're going to give Shaun another shot?"

"Maybe," I said. "You're not going to fall in love with this stalker journalist are you?"

She laughed. "Please, Vic, Ken's just there for the story."

"Yeah," I said, "exactly."

"Come on," she said. "I've got to go meet the band to head to the airport."

"Got everything?" I asked, surveying the apartment. It was a mess, with socks and drinking glasses littered all over the place, but that was the way it always looked. It would've been weird for us to come back to a place that was clean.

We made it downstairs, with the weight of our luggage threatening to send us both flying down the steps, and hailed a cab. I knew that if there had been any chance that we could have carried all our stuff on Mom's bike that she would've tried it, but it really was the only way.

Sooner than we both would've liked, we pulled up in front of Gran's house.

"It's terrible out here," Mom said, getting out of the cab. "You can practically smell the fresh air."

"What a nightmare," I said, hauling my backpack out of the cab's trunk. "By the time you get back, I'll be a foot taller."

"Better hope not, or we'll have to buy your pants at the clown college down the street."

"What are you talking about?" I said, slamming the trunk shut.

"You know? Like those clowns on stilts? Like how they have those super-long pants to cover the stilts? You know what I mean."

"I think it's time for you to go, Mom. Out," I said, pointing with my good hand. "Out of the country, just go."

"Aw, come on. Let me say goodbye to your gran before you banish me from the continent."

"Fine," I said, hoisting my backpack onto my shoulder. "Let's do this."

Mom held up the giant bag from behind as I walked, since it was too heavy for me to carry on only one shoulder.

"It's okay if you hate me, you know," Mom called. "It'll give you fuel for your great novel."

"Who says I'm going to write a book?" I asked.

"Fine then, it'll be fuel for the great shrink I'm sure you'll need in a few years' time."

"You could sell the plane ticket and use the money as a down payment for my therapy bills."

"True," she said. "But I think you can handle this."

"Twenty bucks says I drive Gran up the wall, across the ceiling, and down the other side in the first hour."

"Nah," she said, "keep your money. I'm positive that'll happen."

"My mother the optimist," I said, shrugging off the backpack near the front door.

"Your mother who was raised by that woman." She rang the doorbell. "It's showtime."

Gran answered the door a split second later. "Geez!" Mom said. "You scared us. Were you just waiting for us to ring the bell?"

"Of course," Gran said, smoothing the legs of her tan slacks. They really were slacks, and she insisted on calling them that. "I have nothing better to do with my Sunday than wait by the door for you to arrive."

"I knew it!" Mom said. "Anyway, I'm here to unload this poor orphan child onto your doorstep."

"Hmm, yes," she said, considering me like I was a vacuum cleaner that Mom was selling door-to-door. "Come in, Victoria," she said.

"Thanks, Gran," I said, following her in and dragging the backpack behind me. "You coming, Mom?"

"I better not," she said. "The band's waiting for me. Not to mention the cab driver."

"Oh, right," I said.

It felt like the bottom of my stomach had fallen out, having to say goodbye to her. Even for such an embarrassingly short period of time, relatively speaking. But why did she have to go? Why couldn't she have a normal job like other moms? And why was it so hard for me to say any of this out loud to her?

Instead I hugged her as hard as I could. She hugged me back even harder.

"Michelle, for Pete's sake," Gran said, "you're only going to be away for eighteen days. You'd think you were leaving for good."

And maybe it was something in Gran's callousness or maybe it was just my own embarrassment that had finally caught up to me, but I started to cry.

"Oh, come on, Vic. Don't start. You'll just get me going," Mom said wiping a single tear away. The cab driver honked his horn. "I've gotta go, sweets. I love you."

"Goodbye, Michelle," Gran said. "Have a nice trip."

"Thanks, Mom," she said, letting go of my shoulders. "And thanks for taking care of Vic. You two be good, okay?" She sniffed. "I'll see you both real soon."

"Bye," I said as she gave my shoulder one more squeeze before booking it back to the cab.

It was going to be a long two and a half weeks.

Gran's house smelled like a doctor's office — clean, in a sterile way — and it was pretty obvious from our first morning that we weren't going to be spending a lot of grandmother–granddaughter bonding time together. Gran spent most of her days in her office with the door closed. She had absolutely no interest in me apart from making sure that I didn't die of starvation. She used to be a psychologist. I guess she still is, but she's retired now. She and my grampa met in university back in Halifax. Mom once told me, one night after she'd had a few drinks, that she thought it was weird her mother was so interested in the human brain when she was so bad at dealing with people. Grampa kind of made up for it, though, I guess.

I still miss him.

As soon as I'd unloaded my backpack into Gran's guestroom, I installed myself on the couch. Gran had an ancient TV with basic cable which was kind of a novelty since our place was cable-less, but I was glad I could still watch Netflix once that novelty inevitably wore off — Mom had given me full custody of the computer while she was away. Gran's super-stiff couch hurt my back, though, and it was impossible to get comfortable. I flipped through the channels over and over again but I couldn't focus on anything on the screen.

*It's fine*, I told myself. *It's only two and a half weeks. You'll be home soon and so will Mom. You're being a baby. Mom isn't even in Japan yet, she's barely been gone an hour. Just suck it up, you're being stupid.*

I checked my phone. Mom had been gone for forty-five minutes.

I scrolled through my recent texts. Nothing from Lucy, and nothing from anyone else. I hadn't messaged Shaun in weeks. He'd sent me a text a few days after our disaster date, but I'd been too frustrated with only having one good hand and still reeling from my mortification fest that I hadn't bothered to answer. When I thought about Shaun, all I could remember was how stupid I'd been that day. How dumb I'd been to bring him to a naked beach without even realizing it. I put the phone down.

A few hours and a *Love It or List It* marathon on the W Network later, Gran finally emerged from her office.

"I'm going to make myself an egg-salad sandwich for lunch. Would you like one, Victoria?"

"Oh, nah, that's okay," I said, "I'm not really hungry. And I can't stand mayo."

"What's wrong with mayonnaise?" she asked, giving me a hard stare like I'd told her that I wasn't that into breathing.

"It's nothing. It just kind of grosses me out, that's all. You know, the texture? It's just, like, wrong," I said, getting up from my prone position on the couch.

"Fine," she said, "then you'll have to fix your own lunch. And I hope you're not planning on lying around the house all afternoon. It's a beautiful day outside."

"Yeah," I said, "but with my arm broken there isn't really a lot I can do. Anyway, it's fine, I can make my own sandwich. I don't need you to … I just mean, I can do things myself. And I can choose how I spend my time. Just, like, leave me, okay? Alone?"

"Lunch," she said, launching the words at me like heat-seeking missiles, "and then outside. I'll see you back at seven for dinner."

"Fine," I said, switching the TV off. I tried to muster as much fire in my voice as she had, but Gran had years of experience on her side. My vitriol sounded more like mild annoyance.

I followed her to the kitchen — pastel and linoleum, with a bowl full of wax fruit on the counter — and made myself a bologna and mustard sandwich, the fastest thing I could slap together, while she started methodically cracking and peeling a bowl of hard-boiled eggs she took out of the fridge. Hard-boiling is hands-down the most tragic thing you can do to an egg. It's just so tidy and bland. And then slathering it all in mayo? The thought of it made me want to puke.

I scarfed down my sandwich and put the plate in the sink without a word. I grabbed my phone and my bag from my room and locked the front door behind me, not caring where I wound up. Did Gran really think that wandering the near-suburbs was so much safer than biking downtown? But then I remembered the bookstore with the big yellow sign not far from where she lived, so I turned around and started wandering in its direction.

The store was packed with books and magazines and it was hard to figure out where to start. I walked over to the graphic novel section and scanned the shelves. There were lots that I wanted to look at, but I couldn't focus enough to pick one off the shelf to read. Instead I pulled out my phone.

First I texted Lucy.

*What if each room had a ghost?* I typed with my left index finger, trying to balance my phone on my cast. *And they told you a story as you walked through the house?*

The idea had only occurred to me moments before, but by the time I typed it out I was convinced it was brilliant. Ghosts were exactly what our creepy old house needed.

I stood there for a while looking at my phone, willing Lucy to text me back, but she didn't. I thought about texting Shaun, and hovered my finger over his name on my contact list, willing myself to text him.

*What's left to lose?* I thought, and then typed the only thing I could think of.

*Hey*

I wondered where he was and what he was doing, but I didn't want to ask. I'd been MIA for so long that I figured he'd already forgotten about me. I was sure that he'd filed me away as some weird girl he'd spent an afternoon on a naked beach with and who'd then seemingly disappeared. You know, the usual.

I put my phone back into my bag and tried to forget about it. I told myself that it didn't matter if he texted me back or not. All that mattered was that I had the nerve to finally stop pretending to be invisible. Granted, it took being stranded at a bookstore in the near-suburbs without any friends or a place to go home to until dinner, but still, it felt like a step.

My phone vibrated and my heart felt like it had lost its own instruction manual. I pulled my phone out and saw that I had a message from Lucy and I could feel my whole body unclench.

*Yeah,* she texted, *maybe. We're going to my aunt's house today so I can't work on the game.*

*Oh,* I texted, *that's cool. Tomorrow?*

*My mom, dad and aunt are going away for a few days. I have to stay with Iron Man 1 and Iron Man 2 while they're gone. Not sure when we'll be back but I'll msg you.*

*What happened to Batman and Bane?*

*Guess they needed a new game.*

*So what's up with your parents?* I texted.

*Nothing,* she answered, *just family stuff.*

*Okay, cool. See you soon.*

*If the Iron Men don't kill me first.*

I was browsing through the magazines a few minutes later when I felt my phone vibrate again. I kept flipping through the hipster fashion magazine I had in my hand, trying my best to ignore it. It was no big deal, I told myself. It probably wasn't even Shaun. Probably it was just Gran. Maybe she'd finally figured out how to text with the cellphone Mom bought her for Christmas last year. She just wanted me to come home early, that was all. It definitely wasn't Shaun.

I flipped through more pages of outfits I couldn't afford, and a history of scarves, and when I got to the last page I finally swallowed the sour lump in my throat and looked at my phone. It was Shaun.

*What's up?* he'd texted.

*Bored out of my skull*, I wrote back.

I exhaled loudly enough that a woman nearby look-ing through a home-decorating magazine gave me a dirty look.

*I hear that*, Shaun texted, and I smiled to myself. And to anyone who happened to be looking at me act-ing like a total freak in the magazine section.

*You want to hang out?* I texted.

*Now?*

*Sure, you busy?*

*OK*, he texted. *What do you wanna do?*

And it was all I could do to keep from jumping up and down and hugging Home-Decorating Magazine Lady, who was definitely starting to give me some cut-eye for all the texting I was doing. Like apparently bookstores were supposed to be some sacred, phoneless oasis. But I wasn't about to let her shade bring me down. I felt like a helium balloon rising free into the atmosphere. Shaun still wanted to hang out with me! I hadn't ruined every-thing with the naked beach after all. The only problem was that I had zero date ideas. Especially since the last over-planned one had backfired so spectacularly.

*I'm up for whatever*, I texted him.

*Wanna meet at queen and dufferin in like half an hour?* he answered. *I'm sure we'll think of something.*

*Cool*, I texted, and then bit down on my lower lip to keep from smiling so hard I'd pull a muscle in my cheeks. *See you soon.*

I seriously couldn't believe that had worked. But how was I going to explain to Shaun why I hadn't texted him all this time? And how was I going to tell him how sorry I was for acting like such a weirdo the last time we'd hung out without seeming like a total loser? Fortunately I had pretty well no time to dwell on it. I wasn't even positive that I could get to Parkdale from where I was in half an hour — it would depend on whether or not the luck of public transit was on my side — but I was about to find out.

I hustled out of the bookstore and made a beeline for the closest subway station, Runnymede. I hated not being able to ride my bike, and I still wasn't sure whether or not PYT was going to recover from her injuries since I was too depressed to take her into the shop. Still, the train was fast as we headed east and I caught the southbound bus from Dufferin just as it was pulling out from in front of the station. I could feel my heart in my stomach the whole ride — why was all of this nervousness centred in my gut? Why did falling for someone feel like eating too many nachos? — but we sailed down Dufferin too fast for me to have any second thoughts. When the bus finally spat me out at Queen Street I could hardly believe that I'd made it on time. And that Shaun, his head freshly shaved, was already there waiting for me.

"Uh, hey," I said, stumbling off the high-speed bus and inadvertently landing super close to where he was standing on the sidewalk. He had a bike at his side which was twice as big as the one he'd been riding on the naked beach day. Clearly he wasn't riding his little brother's anymore.

"Hey," he said, smiling at my awkward dismount.

I sniffed. He smelled like weed and sunscreen. I almost laughed at his eau de Coppertone aroma, since Mom and I are always arguing about sunscreen, somehow the smell made him seem less intimidating. We were close enough to hug, but I was grateful that his hands were devoted to holding up his bike so that I didn't have to consider the option. What was this, this thing we were doing? Were we the kind of people who hugged each other? And when was he going to ask about my arm? He was obviously staring at it.

"No bike?" he finally asked.

"Yeah, no," I said. "It's, uh, out of commission. For now."

"Cool," Shaun said. "So ... you wanna go for a walk?"

"Yeah," I said, taking a step back, out of the smelling range. "Sure. Uh, which way?"

"Let's go to Bellwoods," he said, "it's nice there."

"Yeah, okay. Cool. That's, uh, that sounds good."

Trinity Bellwoods was the giant park east of our neighbourhood, a twenty-minute walk away. What were we supposed to talk about on the way there? It was so much easier when we were on our bikes and didn't have a chance to say anything. But I sucked in a nervous breath — the air was hot and it reeked of garbage — and we started walking, Shaun pushing his bike alongside me.

"So," Shaun said, "like, your arm? What happened to it?"

This, at least, was something I could talk about. "Yeah," I said, "it was my bike. I kind of got doored, you know?"

"Seriously?" he said. "That must've hurt like hell."

"Yeah," I said, "it did." But then I panicked. Should I admit that it'd happened right after our first date? Or would reminding him of that day just blow any chance I had left?

"So, like, when did it happen?" he asked.

My mouth started moving before I had time to come up with a lie. "It was that day we went to the, uh, the Island, actually."

"Oh yeah," he said, "that was hilarious."

"So embarrassing," I said, covering my face with my good hand. "I couldn't believe I — well, I …"

"Took us to a naked old-man beach?" Shaun said, filling in my intentional blank. "That was something else, all right. I had fun, though. Those guys were really nice. So what happened?"

He was grinning at me now as we walked along and I could feel my guts turn to jelly — again with the stomach stuff. "I got so … oh god, this is so embarrassing."

"Aw, come on," he said, "it's not that bad."

"No, I was just so, you know, mortified or whatever that I wasn't paying attention on my ride home and I got doored on Queen."

"Damn," he said. "So that's why you never texted me back?"

"Can we just please forget about this?" I asked. "Do over?"

"As long as you let me draw something cool on your cast," he said. "What's it say on there?" He peered to look at what Mom had scrawled.

"Oh, it's nothing," I said. "Just my mom's dumb jokes."

He gingerly grabbed my arm, while still steering his bike one-handed, and started to read. "'Tough break! — Did you see that movie about the broken arm? Great cast! — So much for the right to bare arms!'"

"Ugh, yeah," I said, shaking my head, "she's a real comedian."

"It's kinda cute," he said. "Don't worry, I'll make it look cool."

My face got all hot and red then, which I hoped wasn't noticeable with the heat of the sun threatening to permanently scorch me anyway. I was suddenly jealous of Shaun's Coppertone sheen. Before I knew it, though, we were at the park, and Shaun locked up his bike and then found us a nice and shady spot under a tree near the little valley of the park where people let their dogs run off leash. A tiny chihuahua was running circles around a chubby little bulldog and we sat and watched them for a while as they rolled around and chased each other back and forth.

"C'mere," Shaun said eventually. He pulled a Sharpie out of the backpack he'd been hauling with him and gestured for me to scooch up next to him. I'd been keeping enough distance between us so I didn't pass out from nerves, but I wasn't about to turn down an offer like that. I shuffled forward on the grass to sit beside him, my knee just barely touching his. He traced a finger down my arm — I let out an involuntary shiver — and took my cast in his hands.

I watched as Shaun slowly filled up the empty space of my cast with black psychedelic swirls, skulls, and stars. The only thing keeping me from jumping out of my skin with nerves was that I kept repeating my three-times tables in my head. I tried to make myself breathe slowly and relax, but it didn't really work.

"Yeah," he said, when he'd finally finished. He'd left Mom's cheesy puns alone, but had obliterated the rest of the white space. "That looks good, I think."

"Mhmm," I said, finally finding my voice again. "I really like it. Uh, thanks."

"It's cool. Anyway, I figured your Mom'd be pissed if I covered up her jokes."

"She's not here, actually," I said. "I mean, she's out of town right now. She's in Japan. She's going to be there for a while."

"Oh yeah?" he said. "That's cool. I'd love to see Japan. What's she doing there?"

"She's uh …" Did Shaun not know who my mom was? I'd just figured that everyone at school knew that I was the daughter of a formerly famous musician, even though most of them had never heard of Dusty Moon — it was just the kind of thing that people talked about. If I was completely honest with myself, I'd kind of assumed that Mom was at least part of the reason why Shaun had been into me in the first place.

Shaun stared at me, waiting for me to finish my sentence.

"Business trip," I said, finally. "She's there on business." It wasn't the truth exactly, but it wasn't totally a lie, either. And so what if I wasn't being totally honest? At least for the next two and a half weeks I could be someone other than Micky Wayne's daughter.

"Cool, cool," he said, capping his Sharpie and stuffing it back in his bag. Then he looked back up at me with an expression that could only be categorized as mischievous. "So do you have, like, the house to yourself?"

Another shiver hit me, this time all the way down my spine, which was no small wonder in the August heat. Gran had said that she didn't want me home until seven, and it wasn't like I didn't have the key to Mom's and my apartment. But as soon as I'd thought of it, my heart fell back into my gut. Shaun was beautiful. I wanted to rub my hands all over his buzzed head and hold him as close as my cast would allow, but the truth was that I was kind of scared, too. Kind of really scared. Even though I absolutely wanted to have sex with him. Eventually. But I knew that Shaun had been with a bunch of girls before. He was definitely experienced, and I was so pathetically not. If I took him back to the apartment he'd for sure want to do it and I just wasn't ready yet. The thought of it made me kind of nervous. So nervous that I blurted out, "I'm staying with my gran. She's, uh, she's, like, seventy and a retired psychologist, but she couldn't care any less about me except she needs me to be home for dinner by seven. And it's, uh, what time is it?"

Shaun checked his phone. "Don't sweat it, it's only five."

"Cool," I said, finally exhaling. "Okay, uh, but maybe I should go."

"Oh? I thought maybe we could head over to Rotate That. You know, look at some records? I know it's kind of old school."

"Oh," I said, my sex-nerves quickly dissolving at the suggestion. Record stores I could do, Mom had trained me well. Even as a kid I knew to flip past the used stuff that was scuffed beyond recognition, not to be swayed by jokey album covers, and always be on the lookout for an original pressing of the Rolling Stones' *Sticky Fingers*. We actually went to Rotate That all the time, and they usually recognized me. Well, they recognized Mom, anyway, and me by default. So Shaun's suggestion was totally perfect. I could definitely use a few extra cool-points.

Of course I didn't realize that I'd already paused for too long. "Yeah, sure," I said, fighting a smug grin. "That sounds good."

We walked the two blocks from the park to the record store and went inside. The girl at the front cash was having an animated conversation with a guy who looked about Mom's age. They were both hand-talkers, and you could see them gesturing wildly at each other practically from across the street. I'd seen both of them a bunch of times before, and knew they were friends — or at least big fans — of Mom's. The girl was about seven feet tall with dark purple hair, so I'd always thought she was kind of cool. The guy usually looked like he was try-ing too hard, though, and today was no exception, with a pair of blindingly white Converse special editions and a T that said THIS IS NOT A FUGAZI SHIRT. I don't think he even worked at the store, he just hung out there all the time like he had nothing better to do.

"And I was like 'How many times do I have to tell you it's not in yet?' Dude's in here practically every day, first thing in the freaking morning before I've even had my coffee. I told him, 'Man, you can just give us your number, you know. We'll call you when it comes in. We'll set it aside with your name on it!' but he's all, 'I just love the hunt, you know? I love the hunt.' Like, what is that?"

But as Shaun and I passed by to make our way toward the records in the back, the girl abruptly stopped her story. "Hey!" she said, "It's Vic, right?"

"Yeah, hey," I said, trying to play it cool. "How's it going?"

"Good, man, nice to see you. How's your mom?"

"I hear she's in Japan!" the guy added.

"Yeah, uh-huh. She's fine," I said, before dragging Shaun with me to the back of the store. It was one thing for them to recognize me, but they were totally going to blow my cover before I'd even had a chance to figure out who the new me was. Fortunately, Shaun didn't seem too fazed.

"You're pretty popular, eh?" he said. "What, is your mom in a band or something?"

I could tell he was picturing a middle-aged woman with a desk job who moonlit as a keytar player in a Heart cover band or something.

"Ha-ha, nothing like that," I said, which didn't actually feel like a lie. "She works for a record label," I added, which was almost true. I mean, she was *on* a label. "She just kind of knows a lot of people."

"Wow," Shaun said, "cool."

Fortunately nobody bugged us after that, and we spent close to an hour wandering the aisles and picking up goofy record covers to show each other — breaking one of Mom's cardinal rules, I knew, but I figured that it was okay when there was a boy involved. Neither of us bought anything, and I was relieved to see that the girl at the counter was on her break by the time we left.

We started walking back toward Dufferin, talking about nothing in particular. Shaun suggested we play a game where we each take turns naming a band that starts with the last letter of the band that came before. It took me a couple of turns to get the hang of it, even though we started off pretty easy.

"All right," Shaun said, "let's start basic: The Ramones. So now you've gottta name one that starts with *S*."

My mind drew an unfortunate blank as I stuttered out words that started with *S*, trying to think of a band name. "Snakes, Shoot, Something, Simple, Sleigh. Oh, uh, Sleigh Bells?"

"Heh, yeah, you've got it," he said. "Hmm, *S*? Okay, The Smiths."

We went back and forth like that for a while, until I thought I'd finally stumped him with The Beta Band, an old favourite of Mom's.

"Huh," he said, "don't think I know them. You're not making bands up to try to win, are you? That's a dirty move. You're playing dirty on me, V!"

"I'm not," I said, my hands up in the air in a cease-fire gesture, "I swear!"

"Oh sure, you play all innocent now," Shaun said. "You want another obscure name to follow that up? How about … hmmm, *D*? Uh, lemme think."

An obvious name jumped into my head, but I kept my lips zipped.

"All right," Shaun said finally, "you've probably never heard of them, but I'm using them anyway: Dusty Moon."

I felt a small laugh fighting for life in my throat, but I choked it down. "Oh yeah," I said, "'Stranded in Daylight' and all that? I know those guys."

Shaun's eyes grew hugely wide in surprise and then, before I had a chance to come up with some amazing lie about how exactly I was so well-versed in mid-nineties Canadian alt-rock, he leaned in and kissed me.

Our lips met in a perfect combination of mushy and firm. They tingled. No, it wasn't just our lips. Everything tingled. It was like my whole body was alive with electricity — like a game of Operation gone totally haywire — and I couldn't tell where my mouth stopped and his began.

He was kissing me.

Shaun.

*Shaun.*

And I was kissing him back.

Holy shit!

"Sorry," he said, pulling his mouth away, "I had to."

"You're easily impressed," I said, grinning like an idiot.

"My cousin got me into Dusty Moon when I was a kid," he said. "I totally love them. I can't believe you know them! You're, like, the coolest."

It wasn't as unlikely as Shaun seemed to think. "Stranded in Daylight" was a pretty huge hit, and it still got decent radio play whenever unimaginative DJs got nostalgic about the nineties. But I wasn't about to let him know that.

"Yeah," I said. "I know them pretty well. They were great." Again, not a total lie. "I should, uh, go, though. I mean my gran's going to want me home soon." I pulled out my phone to check the time and saw that Gran had already called three times. Dammit. Fortunately we'd already walked to Dufferin, and I could see the north-bound bus heading up the street toward us.

"Oh, huh," Shaun said, "yeah, sure. I don't want to get you in trouble or anything. But can we, you know, not wait another month until we see each other again?"

"Yeah," I said. "That sounds good." Shaun leaned in for another long kiss. He tasted like sweat and SPF30 which was kind of disgusting but somehow totally perfect. Finally, I pulled away. "That sounds great."

He texted me a minute later as I snagged a seat on the Dufferin rocket:

*You're the coolest.*

It wasn't even remotely true, but maybe I could fake it for just a little longer.

# Nine

I t was weird waking up without Mom around on her birthday, though it wasn't all bad. I was spared the steamroller for one thing, which was a definite plus. Ever since I was little, Mom has started every birthday morning — hers, mind you, not mine — by creeping into my room while I'm still asleep and waking me up by flopping down on my bed and rolling herself over and over me while yelling something like "Birthday steamroller!" or "Mama was a rolling stone!" or even something more elaborate like "How did you know I wanted pancakes for breakfast? Mmmm, freshly steamed!" which doesn't even really make sense. Not that sense has ever been Mom's strong suit.

I've tried to beat her at her own game a few times, but I could never seem to wake myself up early enough to catch her. When I was eleven I'm pretty sure she woke herself up at four in the morning just to get me, crouched in the shadows by my bed, waiting for the deepest part of my sleep cycle to hit. I came pretty damn close to being the world's youngest heart attack survivor that year. Ladies and gentlemen, my mother.

But this year August seventh arrived just like the day before. I woke up in a bed that still felt strange, in the spare room at Gran's house. It was almost eleven, but the house was silent except for the tick-tick-ticking of the clock on the wall next to the bed. It was plain and utilitarian, not a cheesy bird in sight.

I reached under the bed to grab the laptop and turned it on. It started up about as slowly as I did, and I lay back down for a couple of minutes while we each gradually woke up. There was a little lump of guilt in my stomach, about the size of a peach pit from the feel of it, that I hadn't planned anything special for Mom's birthday, even though she was thousands of miles away. We'd hardly talked since she left. I mean, yeah, we'd emailed, but since the time in Japan was fourteen hours ahead of the time here — and she'd been so busy with shows — it'd been hard to find the time to video-chat.

I checked through my overstuffed inbox. I couldn't even remember when she'd suggested we try to talk on her birthday. Scrolling through messages — mostly just spam, exactly how much discount Viagra did the Internet think I needed? — I found Mom's last message. She said we could talk when she got back to her hotel after her birthday-night show. Could I wake myself up early enough to talk at ten in the morning my-time? She said she thought that she could make it back to the hotel by midnight her-time, but that she probably couldn't stay there too long because Mel and the others were going to take her out. The guilty peach pit wobbled and throbbed in my stomach, and I logged on to chat.

She wasn't online, but she'd sent me a series of messages.

> Hey, sweets. Sorry I missed you. Great show in Matsumoto tonight. I couldn't believe everyone knew the words to all my silly little songs. Happy 38th (gasp!!) birthday to meee!
>
> The band's about to drag me off to some bar, and then we're going to a karaoke box or something. I don't really know what the deal is, but you know I'm going to be belting some Prince loud enough that you'll be hearing it back in Toronto.
>
> "Litttttle red corvetttttttte ..."
>
> The tour's going great, though, it's just amazing. And it's great having Ken here. I think he's gotten some good stuff for the book too. I mean, what do I know? But he seems happy with the interviews we've done. He and I are hanging out tomorrow and we're going to do some exploring. We've got the whole day off, which is great, so maybe we can talk then? Miss you (but not toooo much).
>
> xo,
> Mommy Dearest
> Sent: 10:45AM

Of course she couldn't have just waited another ten minutes for me to log on. Like she didn't know how much I usually slept in. Like she didn't know that it had just been a mistake, but that I'd be online soon enough.

It was like she'd done it on purpose. She'd left this tiny little window of her day open for me to slip into, wish her a happy birthday, and then send her off to party with her real friends. Like it was so easy to forget that birthdays were a thing we always did together, only now she didn't have time for me.

And why was she getting so friendly with the leech? This Ken guy was totally suspicious and here she was going off exploring with him, which meant they were probably hooking up by now. Mom always picked the worst guys, and this guy was clearly another premium, grade-A idiot. Couldn't she see that he was just using her to get a better story for his book? He was just another slobbering fanboy and she was eating up his flattery, or whatever it was, with a spoon. A shovel. A forklift.

I wrote her back slowly, hitting one key at a time with the index finger of my good hand.

> Happy birthday. Guess I just missed you.
> Have fun.
> We can talk tomorrow if you can find the time.

And then I closed the computer.

I had to get out of the house, had to get out of the whole neighbourhood. Without my bike I felt trapped. I couldn't move fast enough to put the distance I needed between me and Mom — even if it was just her words on the computer — and Gran's suffocating house. I put my phone and my wallet into my bag and started walking. I made it to the closest subway station, scrounged for some change, and got on the first train headed east.

Without realizing where I was taking myself, I got off at Dufferin, our home stop, and took the bus south to Queen. The bus home.

I checked my phone and realized that Gran had texted me.

*Ill be out for most of the day dinner is at 7 gran*

She really didn't understand how to use her phone. I texted her back to say okay and then started walking. But I didn't know where I wanted to go. I didn't want to go anywhere, really.

I passed Lucy's family's shop and decided to stop in to see if her parents were back in town. Lucy hadn't responded to my texts, but it was possible she'd just left her phone charger at her aunt's house or something. It wouldn't be the first time. I pushed through the door and set off the automatic chime, but the man behind the counter was someone I didn't recognize.

"Hey," I said, "are, uh, Lynn or Walter here?"

"Sorry, no," he said. "Family business. They're out of town."

"Oh, okay," I said. "Thanks anyway."

I was disappointed that things were stalled with Lucy's and my game. As long as she was stuck babysitting in deepest suburbia, we couldn't exactly work on it together. I was excited at the idea of finishing it and showing off to the She Shoots crew, but with Shaun on my mind, the game wasn't really my first priority.

As if on cue, my phone vibrated with a new message. From Shaun.

*Hey*, he texted. *Just thinking about you.*

I knew it was just a matter of time until he figured out who I really was, or, more specifically, who my parents were (had he really not made the connection with my last name?). And it probably wouldn't end well. God, why did he have to be a fan? Still, he was like a super-charged magnet to my heart and I was totally helpless against his pull. I was a little freaked that he'd realize how much I liked him. I knew that the conventional *Cosmo* wisdom was that I had to keep him guessing. To try to cultivate some mystery. So far the only mystery I had going for me was that Shaun didn't know I was the daughter of Dusty Moon, which I was pretty sure was about a million miles from what these manipulative magazine editors had in mind.

I sent Lucy a text to distract myself from more obsession thoughts of Shaun.

*Hey*, I texted, *when you coming home? It's almost my birthday, y'know.*

Then I kept on walking. I'd missed the sights and sounds of Parkdale, since I'd barely been able to breathe on my last date with Shaun, and the noise of neighbourhood personalities clashing in the street. My stomach gurgled as I walked past a row of roti shops, helpfully reminding me that I hadn't actually eaten anything yet that day. I pulled out my wallet and counted my change. When I counted all my loonies and quarters together, along with a couple of nickels, I had just enough.

I ducked into the grungiest of the shops, Roti Lady, where five bucks would buy me enough chicken curry to stretch my stomach to its limit. The sweet woman behind the counter, who probably thought she'd seen my face a bit too often around her shop, wrapped up an extra-large roti for me, and I ate it, tearing off small bits at a time, as I kept walking down Queen, toward the lake.

After crossing over the pedestrian bridge that led down to the water, I climbed up on one of the unattended lifeguard stands on the beach. A couple of dogs were running in and out of the water in an endless game of fetch with their owner, but otherwise the waterfront was pretty quiet. The sun was just starting to set, and the sky was a corally kind of pink. I stuffed the rest of my chicken roti into my mouth, ignoring the pain in my stomach that told me I'd eaten too much, and watched the small waves rising on the sand. The beach was so littered with garbage, cigarette butts, plastic bags, and abandoned flip-flops, that it was hard to forget you were in the middle of the city, but it was still peaceful.

Mom and I used to bring picnics out to the lake and eat them huddled up on the lifeguard stands after the sun went down. We'd done it fairly often the last few summers, but hadn't been down here yet this year. I'd missed it, and I only realized how much as I sat there looking out across the water all by myself.

I thought about Shaun and the way he'd looked right before he leaned in to kiss me, this soft, vulnerable face I'd never seen before. It was beautiful.

And I thought about the game Lucy and I were making, at least in theory.

Things were happening, kind of. Things that Mom wasn't a part of at all. And I felt torn: it was weirdly satisfying knowing that, for the first time, there were parts of my life that Mom knew nothing about, and yet, despite that strange satisfaction, I missed her. Desperately.

My phone vibrated with a text from Lucy.

*So so so sorry*, she texted, *my parents had to extend their trip. I'm stuck in Richmond Hill til Sunday. I'll make it up to you when I get back I promise!! :( :( :(*

I tried to bury my conflicted feelings along with my sinking disappointment as I looked back out onto the water and the swans floating near the shore. At least I still had Shaun around to make my birthday special. I hoped. I balled up the empty roti wrapper and checked my phone.

Damn. Even if I left now I'd still be late for Gran's seven o'clock dinner. Since I was already stuffed and knew that I'd be chewed out anyway, I texted Shaun back.

*Hey you.*

I probably should have waited longer, at least until I had something real to say, but I couldn't hold it in anymore. Why did I have to play dumb just to keep him interested?

I waited a few minutes for another message, but when none came I climbed down from the lifeguard post and started walking back toward Queen. I caught the streetcar up to Dundas West station with the last of my change and texted Gran to let her know that I'd be a bit late.

She texted back, *Dont expect it to be warm when you get her.*

Jesus. At least I had Shaun. And Lucy. And the game. Maybe.

# Ten

nd then a week later it was my birthday. Seventeen. Mom insisted that I set my alarm so we could finally have our belated video-chat first thing when I woke up, and I was more than a bit relieved when she popped up on the laptop's screen wearing a party hat and blowing a noise-maker in my honour.

"Happy birthday!" she yelled, her movements slowed just a bit by the lag in Gran's Internet connection. She was pixelated, too, I guess because Mom's Wi-fi was so weak. She looked like she could have been an anachronistic character from *Lore of Ages II*.

Mom looked happy, but exhausted. She had those dark bags under her eyes that she gets when she hasn't been sleeping enough — visible even in her slow-mo pixelated form — and her hair was even wilder than usual, shooting off in a dozen different frizzy directions.

"Hey, Mom!" I said, waving. "Thanks."

She kept blowing her noise-maker and yelling "Happy birthday!" and "Seventeen!" and "Whoop,

whoop, whoop!" for another full minute before she let either of us finish a proper sentence.

"So how's it going?" she finally said, when she was out of breath from all her merriment. "You giving your gran a hard time or what?"

"Try the other way around," I said. "When she's home, anyway."

"Ah well, that's just her way," Mom said. "But what are you guys doing today? You going to go out for dinner?"

"Not sure," I said, "she hasn't mentioned anything. I'd rather just do my own thing, to be honest."

"But it's your birthday!"

"Yeah, and Gran's not exactly the one I want to spend it with," I said pointedly.

"What about Lucy?" Mom asked.

"She's stuck up in Richmond Hill babysitting her cousins."

"I'm sure she'd love some company," Mom said. And she was probably right. I'd already ignored two texts from Lucy telling me how bored she was. It wasn't that I didn't want to talk to her, but she kept messaging me when I was out with Shaun and I couldn't text her back.

"Yeah," I said, "but I kind of had something else in mind."

"This is about Shaun, isn't it?" Mom asked, totally missing the point.

"It is not," I said. "I haven't even — I don't even …"

"How many times have you guys hung out?" Mom asked.

"A few," I admitted.

We'd been out again since our park/record store/band name game date. We went and saw an old Hitchcock movie they were playing in Bellwoods on a giant inflatable screen. We'd smoked up before it started and the birds that kept killing people in the movie seriously freaked me out, so Shaun kept me distracted by kissing me, first my hand and my neck, but pretty soon we were full-on making out on the grass. Or at least we were until a couple behind us told us to get a room — who even says that anymore? — and I was so paranoid that they'd figured out we were stoned that I told Shaun we had to stop. I confessed that I was a bit of a lightweight as Shaun walked me back to the bus stop afterwards, but he just laughed. "Yeah," he'd said, "I kind of figured."

"Sooooo …" Mom said, "is he taking you out for your birthday?"

"God, Mom, I don't know. Just quit it, okay?"

"Fine, whatever," she said flippantly. "But I'm going to want some details later."

"So how's the tour?" I asked, forcefully changing the subject. "Where are you guys now?"

"Kyoto," Mom said. "We had the day off today, but we'll be playing here tomorrow night, at a place called Urbanguild."

"That's cool," I said. "So what'd you do today?"

"Ken and I did the whole tourist thing. We went to this temple, Ginkaku-ji, I think it's called. Gorgeous. So tranquil, you know?"

"Yeah, I guess." The leech again. Was she spending all of her time with him, or what? "So I guess you really love Japan, huh?"

"Oh, honey, it's great. I've really got to take you here sometime. It's amazing, but it's really kind of overwhelming sometimes. You know, like, everything is strange, just a little bit different from home. The people, the traffic, the music we hear — there's some amazing music here. And the crowds we've had have just been loving our tunes."

"Yeah?"

"Oh yeah. But it's funny. Being here now with the band — you know, the new band, or newish, anyway — it just kind of makes me wish that Dusty Moon had been able to play these shows. It would've been really cool to have done this when we were young. We never made it to Asia."

"Are you thinking about Dennis?" I asked. Was I trying to throw a dart through the love balloon she clearly had forming for the leech? Yeah, I admitted to myself, I probably was.

"Yeah," she said, "I am. Seeing crowds like this makes me miss him a lot. I wish he was here to see this."

But I didn't want the answer I was looking for once I had it. Mom looked a bit misty and faraway over her webcam, but maybe that was just the exhaustion.

And then the screen froze up. It was a sad sort of freeze-frame that almost made me feel sorry for her, stuck and lonesome, even though she was the one out having adventures.

"Mom," I said, "you're cutting out. You're frozen. I can't hear you."

The screen stayed stuck a minute or two longer and then the call was cut off.

I tried redialling her, but it wouldn't let me connect again. It was hard to know what to think of Mom's news. It was great that things were going so well, but it was weird, too. I was too young to remember it back when Dusty Moon was famous, so I've never really known my mom as a big rock star. Was that what she was turning into again?

I went downstairs, still in my pajamas — a giant thrift-store T-shirt with a picture of a cat on the beach and a pair of blue plaid boxers — fully anticipating that Gran would have already left for the day. However it was she spent her days, I had no clue. She was mostly retired, but always seemed to be on her way to a meeting or a conference or something. Or maybe she was just trying to avoid me. In any case, it was pretty surprising to see her actually puttering around the kitchen like she was a normal grandmother who was busy doing something incredibly typical. Like making me a birthday cake?

"You're finally up," she said, as I came into the kitchen.

"Morning," I said. "I was just video-chatting with Mom. You know, for my —"

"Yes," Gran interrupted, "how is she? She's barely able to make time for a phone call."

"Yeah, you know. I mean, she's busy," I said. "She's really busy. She's in, uh, Kyoto, I think she said? Sounds like the tour's going really well. People are really getting into the music."

"I'd hope they would if she's going to fly all that way to play it for them."

"Uh-huh," I said, nodding as I scanned the kitchen

counter for a present, or even a card, that I might have missed. Maybe I just hadn't given her the right opening to wish me a happy birthday? "So …"

"So," Gran said, "what are your plans for the day?"

"Well …" I paused, sure she'd catch herself. But then the pause went on for too long and I felt like a moron. "I mean … it's my birthday."

"Of course it is," she said. "You didn't think I could forget that, did you?"

"Oh," I said, stalling further, waiting for an uncharacteristic hug or even some impersonal present like a GAP gift card.

"Yes," she said, touching my arm. "Happy birthday. You're how old now?"

"Seventeen," I said, slumping my shoulders. Gran took her hand away. There was no hug here. No gift card. Probably not even a stupid birthday card.

"Ah, yes," she said. "You're growing up. And I'd be happy to make you a birthday dinner here tonight if you'd like. You could invite a friend."

And it wasn't like I was some spoiled reality-TV-show brat, but Gran's pathetic offer to heat up some frozen fish for me and one friend — Lucy was still baby-sitting in Richmond Hill, and there was no way she'd even let Shaun into the house — was the total opposite of how I'd pictured my birthday.

"No thanks," I said, "I've got other plans."

I was shocked to see Gran look disappointed that I'd turned down her offer. The corners of her mouth fell, but she nodded her head.

"Fine," she said. "So where are you planning to have dinner tonight?"

"My friend Lucy invited me," I heard myself say, "for a sleepover."

"And it's all right with her parents?"

"Yeah, Gran, it's fine," I said. "It's, like, a birthday sleepover. We did one for Lucy's birthday too, back in February."

"And your mother knows about this?"

God, I was going to get caught in a lie for sure. Fortunately, Mom was probably already off doing shots and singing karaoke with the leech, and there was no way Gran could get ahold of her before tonight, tomorrow morning her-time.

"Yeah," I said, "it's fine. We do it a lot. It's no big deal."

"Okay," she said. "But be back early tomorrow. I don't want you to overstay your welcome."

"Fine, whatever," I said, grabbing a banana from the fruit bowl on the counter — which sat next to the bowl of wax fruit, Gran seriously had no idea how to decorate — and went back up to the spare room. I threw some stuff into my bag, and then headed for the door, texting Shaun before I'd even reached the end of the block.

*I'm coming over. OK?*

By the time I'd hit the bank so that I actually had subway fare to get back downtown, Shaun had replied.

*My parents are going out tonight. Come over after 8. They'll be home late.*

I was bummed that he didn't want to spend the day together. Eight o'clock felt like it was days away, but his message sent a shock through my body and I broke out in all-over goosebumps. This was it. This was what I wanted. I was going over to Shaun's. I'd convince him to let me stay over — something told me that it wouldn't be too hard — and we'd, well, do it. That was what Shaun did with girls, he'd been with enough of them. And I wanted to. With him.

It was totally fine. It made sense. I really liked him and it was my birthday.

My seventeenth birthday.

My seventeenth freaking birthday with my mom on the other side of the world, and Lucy stuck in the suburbs babysitting while I was being babysat by Gran, who didn't even give enough of a crap about my special day to buy me a grocery-store birthday cake with pink frosting.

*Yup, this is it*, I told myself as I pushed through the turnstile at the subway station. *I'm going to sleep with Shaun. No, not "sleep with" — how old was I, Mom's age?* — I was going to have sex with Shaun. For sure. I mean, he was practically my boyfriend now anyway.

*God*, I thought, as I boarded the train. *Was he my boyfriend?* It was kind of hard to tell. We'd hung out a few times, and we'd made out a whole bunch, sure, but was he my boyfriend? Then I had a worse thought: was he hanging out, and making out, with other girls, too? It was at least a possibility, and the thought of it made my stomach squeeze itself tight like it was trying to turn the sad banana I'd had for breakfast into a diamond.

I decided to head to the Eaton Centre downtown, and in between the people-watching and the consolation birthday shopping I did — including some new underwear that I immediately changed into in the mall's food court bathroom — I managed to keep myself distracted, even if it was a pretty pathetic way to spend the day.

I parked myself near the fountain in the middle of the mall for almost an hour and drew weird little left-handed portraits of the people around me in a new sketchbook I'd decided was a birthday necessity. Once I gave in to how childish my left-hand drawing was, it was actually kind of fun to see how distorted my portraits came out — how grotesque they made the pretty people around me look. And for once it didn't feel like I was doing it wrong, or that my art wasn't good enough — I was just enjoying drawing. For the first time, I realized, in a while.

When I got tired of the mall, I crossed Dundas Square and went to the movie theatre across the street. I'd never gone to a movie by myself before, but I figured that I didn't have much choice since I still had a few hours to kill before I could head over to Shaun's place. I got a ticket to *Pure Joy*, a horror movie Shaun was obsessed with about a summer camp run by a cult, and bought myself a giant bag of popcorn, a bucket of Coke, and a pack of Junior Mints. I figured that if no one else was going to buy me a birthday dinner that I'd just have to be my own date.

The movie was freaky but so good, and my popcorn/Junior Mint/Coke dinner was about the best meal I'd ever eaten, mostly because I was so hungry. When the credits finally rolled, and I dug my nails out of the armrests, I checked my phone and realized that it was close to eight. Time to head over to Shaun's.

I walked down to Queen to catch the streetcar and grabbed a single seat by the window. My nerves, which I thought I'd managed to completely exorcise with my day of distraction, came back in full force as I watched Queen Street whip by. As we got closer to Lansdowne Avenue, Shaun's stop, I was convinced that I'd somehow pissed myself, I was sweating so hard — everywhere, but especially between my legs. Who knew that you could even sweat there? I was mortified, and made a note to make sure that I cleaned myself up in Shaun's bathroom before letting him get close.

The thing was that I really liked Shaun. I did. He was gentle with me. He was sweet, when he wasn't making fun of me for being a lightweight. He asked me questions and laughed at my jokes and was for sure the only guy I knew who regularly wore sunscreen.

*You invited yourself over*, I thought to myself as we cruised along a lot faster than I would have liked. You invited yourself over, so he's going to think that you want to have sex with him. That you're ready.

*Are you ready?* I asked myself as I rang the dinger and got off the streetcar.

*Are you ready?*

I had absolutely no idea.

# Eleven

I walked as slowly as I could, but still, a few minutes later I wound up at Shaun's door. I'd been there once before. When he and I were in the same drama group at school we'd rehearsed our one-act play at his place. It was me, Alexis, this girl Allison who acted like she was too good for everything, Shaun, and a stoner friend of his, Sammy, who was so perma-baked that he couldn't even open his eyes all the way. We'd done a modern retelling of *Alice in Wonderland*, where Alice goes a party and gets roofied. It didn't make a ton of sense, which I guess is what happens when five people try to write a play all together.

I recognized the Christmas wreath that looked like Santa's head hanging on the door. The wreath had been appropriate enough when we'd met to practise our play back in December, but now it seemed more than a little unseasonal, even though someone had taken the care to stick a little pink cocktail umbrella into Santa's beard. I stared at that tiny umbrella, willing my heart to slow to less than a million beats per minute before I knocked on the door.

When I finally realized just how long I'd been standing there, I rang the bell. A minute later, a little boy, about nine or ten, answered the door. He had to be Shaun's brother, with matching red hair and freckles he looked almost exactly like a mini-Shaun, minus the shaved head.

"Shaun's upstairs," he said, opening the door just enough for me to squeeze my way inside.

"Cool. Thanks," I said, bending down to unzip my four-years-old knee-high gladiator sandals. They'd belonged to one of Mom's friends originally, who paid too much for them when they were first in style. They'd only been handed down to me once they'd been worn practically to death, but I figured there was a decent chance the style would come back in again eventually since it seems like nostalgia is the new black these days. Besides, they still looked kind of sophisticated and cool, even if they were on their last legs. Or, at least they would have, if the zipper hadn't gotten stuck halfway down.

The right sandal came off, no problem, but I was midway down my calf when the zipper refused to budge any further on the left.

*No biggie*, I thought, zipping downward with slightly more force, and wishing I had two good hands to work with. Nothing. I tried to press the zipper tight at the top with my cast and tugged even harder down with my right hand, but still the stupid thing wouldn't move. I started to panic and tugged the zip tab up, hoping to unstick it, but the flimsy piece of metal broke off in my hand. I shoved the little tab into the pocket of my shorts — cutoffs that were, I only noticed then, riding up on my thighs. I quickly adjusted them, hoping that mini-Shaun wasn't looking, and then started trying to jiggle my foot free of its sandal prison.

Why the hell had I worn these things today? They only made my calves look bigger, I realized now. In them, I was practically a mutant. And the straps seemed to tighten around me the more I tried to shake them loose. Which I realized was totally impossible, but didn't stop the vision I had of having to amputate my foot just to get me out of these stupid sandals.

"You down there, V?" Shaun called down a minute later when I still hadn't gone upstairs to meet him.

"Yeah," I said, with more than a hint of anxiety in my voice. "Just, uh, my, uh … just give me a minute."

Mini-Shaun finally looked up from the couch where he was parked to stare at me. "I don't think that's how you're supposed to do it," he said.

"Thanks for the advice," I said, as a bead of sweat rolled from my forehead down to my chin. "Can you —?" I asked, pointing to my foot.

"What?" his eyes were back on the screen. I only realized now that he had a PlayStation controller in his hands.

I'd reached peak embarrassment with my horrible hand-me-down gladiators and didn't care anymore about trying to play it cool. "Could you come here and pull this thing off my foot?"

"Fine," he said, not at all fazed by the request. He paused his game and lumbered over to me, his feet landing heavy on the shiny hardwood floors as he dragged himself over like a bear who'd been shot with a tranquilizer dart.

"Thanks," I said, sitting down on the floor and stretching out my foot. "Just pull."

"This thing's like a prison for feet," he said, eyeing the dozen or so straps running up my leg.

"Yeah, exactly," I said. "So, on three, all right?"

"Whatever."

"Okay," I said. "One, two …"

Shaun appeared at the landing looking down just as I called out "three." He was halfway to saying something like "What?" or "Huh?" when mini-Shaun wrenched the sandal prison from my foot. The leather straps dragged across my skin, leaving bright-red chafe tracks behind them.

"Ow!" I tried to stop myself from crying out, but the sound was out of my mouth before I'd even realized what was happening.

"Whoa," Shaun said. He'd somehow made it down the stairs in the time it took his brother to pull the offending footwear off of me. "You okay?"

"Uh-huh," I said in a tiny, squeaky voice, "no problem. Thanks, uh …"

"Miles," Shaun said, nodding at his brother, who'd already reclaimed his spot on the couch. "That looks like it hurts. Your foot, I mean."

"Nah. It's cool, really," I said, even as the red scrape marks on my foot throbbed even brighter.

"Let me get you, like, something medicinal." He smiled and walked back toward what I assumed was the kitchen.

I wondered if I should follow him or if that would make me look too clingy. I decided to hang back. I'd just barely recovered from the sandal incident, I reasoned, and needed a second to relax just to keep from bursting out in stress-hives. I walked halfway and then paused to check out what game Miles was playing. It was an RPG I didn't recognize.

"Mind if I watch?" I asked, sitting down on the arm of the couch where he'd stationed himself.

"Whatever," Miles said, not taking his eyes off the screen.

"Hey," Shaun called, "do you like gin? It's, like, all my parents have."

I'd never had gin. It seemed kind of like an old-lady drink, but I definitely wasn't going to say no. I was glad I'd finally weaned myself off my painkillers since I could still hear Mom's lecture about my night with Lord Windermere in my head.

"Uh-huh," I said, "sure, that's cool. Oh, I almost forgot, I saw *Pure Joy*!"

"Oh man," Shaun said, popping his head out into the living room. "Did you love it? It's so good."

"Oh my god, yeah," I said. "So freaky. It was awesome."

"Totally," Shaun said, ducking back into the kitchen.

I looked back at Miles's game.

"What are you playing?" I asked.

"*Dragonfury Infinite*," Miles said, and I realized I'd heard of the game before.

"Oh yeah, cool. That's an Archford game, right?" I said, naming the same developer that made *Lore of Ages*.

"Uh-huh," he said, his eyes never leaving the screen. If that trivia had scored me any points with him, he wasn't showing it.

Shaun came back into the living room with two drinks in his hands. "Gin and juice," he said, handing me what looked like a tall glass of OJ.

"Now remember, Miles. It was, like, the gin goblins that took it, okay?"

I laughed, but then I started looking around the living room. The whole place was stacked with old books that were practically falling all over each other. It'd been tidier the last time I'd been here, but I liked the mess better. The whole place had a scatterbrained-professor vibe to it now, and it relaxed me.

"You want to take these upstairs?" Shaun asked, elbowing me gently in the side.

"Sure," I said, "sounds good."

Shaun ruffled his brother's hair. "Our secret, right?"

"Whatever," Miles said, turning his full attention back to the game.

"All right," Shaun said, gesturing toward the stairs. "Let's go. Oh, maybe you should take your sandals with you, you know? I'll, uh, grab your drink."

"Oh yeah," I said, forgetting for a moment that I was supposed to be an invisible visitor.

I grabbed my busted gladiators and followed him

up, staring at the back of his head and his shirt as he climbed the stairs. His hair was growing in again, a little fuzzy crop of orange that stood out all around his head. He was wearing some goofy shirt from a bait and tackle shop in Florida. The back had a giant marlin wearing sunglasses with the tagline MASTER BAIT (& TACKLE). He'd cut the arms off and his biceps and the back of his neck were speckled with freckles and sweat.

The house was definitely warm, it was one of those old Toronto houses that didn't have air-conditioning. It made me feel a little less bad about the fact that our tiny apartment is always such a sweat box.

He turned around when we got to the top of the stairs. "Oh man, I totally forgot to say it. Happy birthday!"

"Thanks," I said, turning almost as red as my feet had been a few minutes before.

"Come on," Shaun said, leading me into the second bedroom on the left, "this is my room."

I walked in and he shut the door behind me. And it wasn't that I wasn't expecting him to, but there was something about the little click as he closed the door that seemed definitive and maybe just a little bit terrifying. His walls were covered in posters layered on more posters — bands and movies — and behind them I could see that his walls were painted a dark teal.

He sat down on his bed — it wasn't made, the covers lay somewhere in a pile at the foot of it — and he patted the spot beside him. The bed looked like sex, and so did he, and I put my sandals down on the floor and climbed in after him. *It's fine*, I told myself. *It's totally fine. This is what everyone does. Mom's done it, and so has Gran. Just sit down.*

He put his arm around me and kissed the top of my head. "Oh, wait," he said, scrambling to get up. "I almost forgot your birthday present." He rummaged around in the drawer of his desk across the room. The desk itself was so piled with crap — dirty clothes and empty bags of chips — that it was impossible to imagine that he ever sat down and worked there. "It's here somewhere," he said. "Oh yeah, here it is!" He held a card that looked completely handmade high in the air for me to see.

"This is for me?" I asked. It was covered with magic-markers scribbles and looked more like a toddler had made it then a sixteen-year-old guy. Apparently Shaun had been practising his regressive art style, too. "What is this, child labour?"

"You like it?" he asked proudly. He'd drawn a teddy bear holding a bunch of balloons with HAPPY 17TH BIRTHDAY, V!!!! scrawled over top of it all.

"It's perfect," I said, laughing. "You're such a weirdo."

"It took you this long to figure it out?" he asked.

"What can I say? I'm a slow learner."

"So … open it!" he said impatiently. He really was acting like an over-sugared preschooler. Kind of like Mom, actually. Was this really all for my benefit?

I opened the card and two tickets fell out. For some show, I assumed. Some super obscure band he knew I'd love because of course I was *so cool.* How much longer was it going to be before he figured out that I really wasn't?

I picked them up from where they'd landed the bed.
FAN CON CANADA: SATURDAY GENERAL ADMISSION
No. Way.

I was going to Fan Con.

I really was. With Shaun.

"Are you serious?" I said, my eyes practically bugging out of my head.

"You ever been? It's, like, the coolest thing." He stopped himself. "I mean, it's pretty cool. Like a million people go. There's comic stuff and gamer stuff and horror stuff." It was his chance to turn red. "It's kind of nerdy, I know. But I thought you might want to go with me."

Tickets to the biggest convention in Canada. For my seventeenth birthday. From my dream guy.

"Yeah," I said, "that sounds …" It sounded perfect. "That sounds pretty all right." I couldn't fight the goofy smile that was spreading across my face. "I'll totally go nerd out with you. That sounds awesome."

"Happy birthday," he said again, putting his arm around me and slowly guiding us both into lying down on his bed. He was warm, he was so warm it was almost too much.

And everything about the moment was perfect, especially Shaun. He rubbed my arm, and I nuzzled my head under his chin as he purred, cat-like, but I still felt on edge.

"Is it okay if we don't have sex?" I blurted out.

"Huh?" he said, sitting up to look at me.

"I don't … I mean, the tickets are amazing. Really, it's so sweet. And I don't want to go home or anything — I can't, seriously — but, like," I took a deep breath, "I just don't think I'm ready. I don't want to have sex with you. Tonight, I mean. I do, like, eventually. Just not tonight, okay?"

"Oh," he said. "Okay. I mean, that's cool. You can still stay over. But, um, is there anything I could do to make you, you know, change your mind? It is, like, your birthday and all."

"Yeah," I said, staring down at my now mostly healed feet, tucked up on the bed near a discarded T-shirt. "I know."

"And you liked the card, right?" he asked hopefully.

"Of course," I said, "it was so sweet. Nobody's ever made me a card like that before."

"And they never will," he said. "That's a limited edition of one."

"It's perfect," I said. "And I really like you."

"Yeah?" He sounded surprised, and I wondered if I'd said too much.

"Yeah," I said, trying to will myself to maintain whatever allure I had left. "I just … it's me. I'm not ready." I realized that it was the truth the second the words left my mouth, even though I really wanted to be.

"Oh," he said. "Okay."

"Plus, like with my arm and everything. I just … I think maybe we should wait until my cast comes off, you know?"

"Yeah," he said. "I mean, like … yeah, okay. Whatever you, you know, need. It's cool."

"Thanks," I said. And I meant it.

"I really like you, too, you know," he said, looking away from me. "You're, like, the coolest girlfriend I've ever had."

Girlfriend.

*Girlfriend.*

The word sounded utterly amazing.

"You're not so bad yourself," I said.

I leaned my head against his shoulder and he turned back toward me and kissed my forehead. Then he reached into the drawer of his bedside table and pulled out a baby joint and a lighter.

"You wanna just, like, watch a movie on my laptop?"

"Yeah," I said, "that'd be great."

"It's kinda hot, though. You mind if I take off my shirt?"

"Be my guest," I said, smiling.

And he was right, it was way too sweltering, even with the window open, for us to be completely dressed.

Shaun took off his shirt and I slid out of my cutoffs so I was lying in his bed in just my shirt and brand-new bright purple underwear. And my cast, of course. He gave me a big hug and kissed the top of my ear before pulling out his computer.

And we lay there, with me cuddled up on his chest, forcing myself to breathe in and out. In and out. In and out.

And it was kind of perfect.

# Twelve

I didn't even realize I'd fallen asleep like that, curled up on Shaun's chest — two and half movies, one gin and juice, and half a joint later — until the alarm on my phone went off at six the next morning. I was glad I'd at least had the foresight to make sure that I got myself up in time so that I wouldn't get caught sneaking out of the house. Shaun's parents had come home pretty late. Late enough that they didn't bother checking in on him, and for that I was incredibly grateful.

Shaun didn't seem to hear my alarm, or at least he chose to ignore it, so I slunk around his room gathering up the few things I'd brought with me. I folded his preschool-style birthday card in half and tucked it into my bag.

The Con was next week and we were going.

Together.

And I was Shaun's girlfriend.

*Girlfriend.*

His girlfriend whom he hadn't slept with yet, and which he was apparently cool with. At least until my

cast came off, anyway. I looked back down at my sandals. There was no way I was going to be able to wrestle
them back onto my feet, especially with a broken zipper.
What was I going to do, go home barefoot?

I slunk back over to the bed and kissed Shaun to
wake him up, still hardly believing that this was where I
was, and that this was what I was doing.

"Hey," I whispered, "I better, uh, get going, you
know? Before your parents wake up."

"Hey," he croaked, turning over to face me. His
eyes barely opened, but they were still the most beautiful things I'd ever seen, with a little gold ring around
his pupils that I'd never noticed before. He looked so
peaceful lying there, defenseless. I really didn't want to
go. Like, seriously. I could have lived in those eyes for a
long, long time.

"Hey," I said again, sitting down next to him on the bed.

"I'm really glad you stayed over," he mumbled, apparently too tired to sit up.

"Yeah?"

"Oh yeah," he said, nodding dozily.

"Hey, uh, do you have any, like, flip-flops I could borrow?" I asked. "I can't exactly wear my sandals home."

"Oh, yeah, right," he said, smiling. "I've got a pair
under the bed you can borrow."

I got down on my hands and knees and peered
underneath the bed where I still couldn't believe I'd
spent the night.

Amidst the tumbleweeds of dust and boy hair were
a grungy pair of flip-flops. They'd clearly been black at

some point, but in their current caked-in-grime and sun-baked state they were more of a greyish brown. I fished them out with one hand and tried them on. They stuck out two inches in the back, but they'd have to do.

"They look good on you," Shaun teased as I inspected my hilariously tiny-looking feet.

"Maybe I'll keep them," I said, tapping my feet lightly on the floor.

"Maybe I'll let you."

He pulled me in for another kiss. His morning breath was disgusting, but I didn't mind. Well, maybe just a little.

"Anyway," I said when we finally came up for air, "I should get going. Text me later?"

"I'll think about it," he said, turning over onto his side. "Just be quiet when you leave, okay?"

"Obviously," I whispered, kissing him on top of his fuzzy head.

"I like it when you do that," he mumbled, and then promptly started snoring.

Sneaking out of a boy's house first thing in the morning was brand-new territory for me, and the house itself seemed to have something against me from the start. There was no way the floor had been so creaky the night before. Though I was at least smart enough to carry Shaun's massive flip-flops with me instead of wearing them down the stairs. Their soft *fwip-fwip-fwipping* would have given me away for sure. Still, I couldn't figure out if I'd make less noise walking fast or slow, so I compromised by taking long, slow steps as I made my way toward the stairs.

Naturally, each step seemed to be squeakier than the last — I guess all the heat had made the hardwood floor swell or something — and it was a miracle that I made it down to the main floor without any strange parental heads popping out of the master bedroom.

I was about a foot away from the front door when I finally heard a noise.

"Hey."

I looked up. Miles was still sitting on the couch in the living room, looking like he'd hardly moved an inch since we'd seen him there the night before.

"Oh. Hey," I stage-whispered, pointing at the door. "I was just, you know, leaving."

"Right," he said, at full volume. He wasn't exactly helping me keep up my stealth act.

"Just, like, don't tell your parents I was here," I said. "All right?"

"Yeah," Miles said, finally lowering his voice, "our moms'll freak if they see you."

"Oh, yeah," I said. Was it weird that Shaun hadn't mentioned his parents were gay? Did he think that I'd care or something? I didn't have long to think about it, though, because, as if on cue, I started to hear voices coming from upstairs.

"You've gotta go," Miles said, getting up from the couch and practically pushing me out the front door. I grabbed my bag and Shaun's flip-flops and Miles turned the bolt on the door behind me just as I started to hear footsteps coming down the stairs. After nearly tripping on the giant rubber sandals, I started walking as fast as I could manage toward the bus stop, turning around at the end of every block to check over my shoulder for stampeding parents.

It looked like seventeen was going to be a lot more interesting than I'd imagined.

My head was still spinning as I caught the bus and rode the subway back to Gran's place, and it wasn't until I was nearly at her door that I realized I should probably tone down the goofy smile I was sporting. It was bound to give me away. I practised looking solemn and sleepy as I flip-flopped my way back to her house, and was surprised when she opened the door for me just as I was fitting my key into the lock.

"You look tired," she said. She was dressed in her customary tan slacks, but was wearing a plain white T-shirt with them. She looked practically ready for the beach by Gran standards.

"Yeah," I said, trying to somehow cover up my feet so she wouldn't ask questions, "you know … sleepover and everything."

But all the shuffling of my feet only seemed to attract her attention. "Whose sandals are those?" she asked, pointing at the rubber surfboards I'd shuffled home in.

"Oh, they're, uh, Lucy's dad's," I said. "I broke mine last night and he lent me his."

"They couldn't lend you a pair that fit?"

"I guess this was just, like, the only extra pair they had."

"Strange," Gran said, looking hard at Shaun's flip-flops like she didn't quite believe me.

"Can I come inside now?" I asked, trying hard to change the subject.

"Oh. Well, I thought," she cleared her throat, then paused and fished a cough drop out of her pocket, "I realized that I wasn't being quite fair to you yesterday."

"You mean the fact that you basically ignored my birthday?"

Mom had told me over and over not to be short with Gran, that she didn't take it well, but if it hadn't been for Shaun, and Miles, for that matter, I would have had the most pathetic seventeenth birthday ever, thanks almost entirely to Gran. I was in no mood to pull my punches.

Her face darkened, and for a second I thought for sure she was going to tell me off for insubordination or whatever. She sucked harder on her cough drop and pursed her lips. "You and I clearly have very different views on birthdays. And I'm —" she coughed "— sorry if you felt that I wasn't paying you enough attention on your special day. I know that you and your mother generally celebrate your birthdays together, so I can imagine —" she coughed again "— that this may be a bit hard on you."

"Uh-huh." Strangely enough, Gran seemed like she was actually trying to offer up an apology, but that everything, even her lungs, was trying to keep her from it.

"I thought maybe I could make it up to you." She coughed again and cleared her throat. "By taking you out for breakfast." She cleared her throat again. Exactly how much mucus did she have rattling around, anyway?

"Seriously?" I asked.

"Yes, of course," she said. "What do you say?"

Apparently seventeen was full of surprises.

"Yeah," I said, "sure. Just, um, let me get changed, okay? I'll just be a minute."

"Fine," she said. "I'll wait for you here."

I waddled my way into the house in a bit of a daze. I changed out of my cutoffs, T-shirt, and day-old underwear as quickly as I could with my one good arm and pulled the one sundress I'd brought with me over my head. I twisted my hair up into a top knot — which took nearly fifteen minutes, it was surprising how hard it was to make a bun one-handed — stuck on some fresh deodorant and met Gran back outside. She'd been just standing there, staring at traffic.

"You look nice," she offered, as I locked the door behind me.

"Thanks," I said. "You, too. So where do you want to go?"

"Something casual, I thought. Is the Sunset Grill all right?"

The fact that she wanted my opinion was almost as shocking as the fact that she was taking me out for a post-birthday breakfast in the first place. That, and the fact that she was wearing the closest thing she owned to a leather jacket and ripped denim. I ignored the fact that it was only just after seven in the morning and that I probably wouldn't even be hungry for another couple of hours and said, "Yeah, sure, that sounds great."

We walked in relative silence to the restaurant, which was fine by me since I seemed to be developing some kind of time-delayed hangover, even though I'd only had one very strong drink the night before. I felt a headache starting to throb just underneath my forehead and focused on putting one foot in front of the other until I'd eventually have a coffee and a tall glass of juice — hold the gin — in my hand.

When we got there, a woman who was way too perky for seven in the morning sat us at a table by the window. I had to gulp down a pint of water before I could even look at the menu.

"Are you all right?" Gran asked, glancing up from her menu. "You look ill."

"Thanks a lot," I said, crunching on the last bits of ice at the bottom of my glass.

"Would you like a cough drop?" Gran asked, offering her roll of Halls to me before stopping herself. "Never mind, I don't have enough to share."

She still had half a pack left and her cough seemed to have disappeared altogether, but I knew this wasn't a fight worth picking. "I'm good," I said, with a certain amount of force. "Just tired."

"Well," Gran said.

"Well what?"

"You're well," she said, taking off her glasses for emphasis, "you're not good."

I took an extra-large pull from the steaming mug of coffee that seemed to have materialized entirely from my intense desire for caffeine. I enunciated my words slowly and clearly. "If I say I'm good, then I'm good."

"You're well," she said, putting her glasses back on and sipping carefully from her own glass of grapefruit juice.

"I'm hungry," I said, finally quelling whatever weird grammar fight was brewing. "And I'm having waffles."

I pointed at a picture on the menu of a giant golden waffle. Then my eye caught the picture below. "No," I said, stabbing at the picture of a massive Belgian waffle covered in strawberries and whipped cream with my finger. "I'm having the Sunset Waffle Supreme."

A snarky comment of some kind — about my weight, maybe, or about having a mountain of whipped cream for breakfast, or even at the crassness of my aggressive pointing — nearly crossed her lips, I could tell. I could practically see it bubble up on her tongue and then, just as quickly, she swallowed it.

"Hmm," she said. "That looks ... good."

"So you'll have one, too?" I asked, pushing her patience.

"No," she said, shaking her head as if to banish the vision of cream and berries from her mind. "I'm having a Western omelette."

Our perky server returned as we closed our menus in front of us.

"Yum!" she said, as I ordered my over-the-top waffle sundae. "Great choice!" And I nodded smugly at Gran as if this poor woman, who was paid minimum wage to be so over-the-top encouraging of people's poor choices, had somehow validated mine.

Our food arrived and we ate mostly in silence, which was clearly the only way we were going to avoid a fight. I got up to use the bathroom — drowning my hangover in whipped cream hadn't been the best choice, as it turned out — and sat in the slightly grimy little stall willing my headache to end. I read the graffiti on the stall's walls and door:

*GC+SS 4ever*

*They only love you til you can't give them anymor*
*KC is a sexy scientist <3*

Turning to flush, I realized that the last person to leave their mark on this unsuspecting bathroom door had left their weapon of choice behind on top of the toilet tank: a black Sharpie.

I uncapped it and then paused. I wrote:

*never underestimate the power of a pair of borrowed flip-flops*

And underneath, in tiny letters, *happy 17 to me.*

Lucy texted me just as Gran was paying our bill to say that she was finally home, and I booked it straight over to her house from the restaurant. It was close to ten by the time I got there, but it was still a whole lot earlier than I usually invited myself over. Her house was unusually messy, with boxes stacked up all over the place.

"How were Iron Man 1 and Iron Man 2?" I asked, as we settled into her parents' office.

"Ugh, don't remind me," Lucy said. "I hate babysitting."

"And it was just you and your little cousins?" I asked, impressed that her parents had trusted her to supervise.

"My cousin Eric was there, too. He's twenty-five, but he still lives at home. So technically he was the adult, I guess, but I was the one doing all the work. Those kids are disgusting."

"That sucks," I said. "Why were your parents out of town?"

"It's my grandma. They had to help her move out of her house and into an old folks' home."

"Oh," I said.

"Yeah. I guess cleaning her house out took them a lot longer than they thought. It's all piled up here now, that's why our house is such a mess."

"It's not that bad," I said. "Anyway, it's not any worse than our place is."

"True," said Lucy, "but I'm still hoping we can get rid of this stuff soon."

"For sure," I said. "Oh! I almost forgot to tell you. Shaun got us tickets to Fan Con!"

"Whoa," she said, "he paid for your pass?"

"Not all four days, just for the Saturday. Still, I'm so excited!"

"That's still a lot of money," Lucy pointed out. "He must be expecting something pretty big in return."

"It's not like that," I said, "It was a birthday present. Why are you being weird about this?"

"Sorry," she said, "whatever. It's cool. We can all hang out together on Saturday."

"Totally," I said, as I mentally calculated the odds of Shaun getting along with Lucy and her friends. They weren't great.

"Anyway," Lucy said, turning on her parents' computer and tapping the monitor, "let me show you your birthday present."

"Huh?" I said, as she pulled up Twine and loaded our game. It looked different than I remembered. She'd added a goofy drawing to the first page.

"It's finished!" Lucy said proudly.

But my face was stuck in neutral. "Oh," I said. "Cool."

"Check it out," Lucy said. "I added art and every-thing. Behold *Castle Forkenstein!*"

I started to click through. The illustrations that Lucy had added were kind of cheesy, but it was cool that she'd figured out how to put them in. "But how did you do this from your aunt's place?" I asked. "I thought we could only works on the game from here?"

"I just installed Twine on her computer and trans-ferred the file," Lucy said. "It was easy. But, anyway, do you like it? Isn't it great?"

It was cool seeing the game finished, but it really wasn't what I'd had in mind when we started. Lucy had made the game funny. *Castle Forkenstein* was about finding recipes in the deserted manor of a vampire chef. But I'd wanted to tell a ghost story. A real one. And I'd wanted to be the one to illustrate it. Though, admittedly, I'd never mentioned that to Lucy.

"It's cute," I said. "But weren't we going to make it, you know, scary?"

"Funny is better," Lucy said, "we'll stand out this way. Plus, it's about food, so we can totally present it at the next She Shoots social."

"Huh?"

"I texted you about it. The social's where people give presentations about the games they've made. So since their game jam was all about food, I figured this would fit right in! I've already emailed them to ask."

"But that's not, like, the game I wanted to make," I said. "That's not what we've been working on."

"I just kind of figured you weren't interested anymore

179

since you started ignoring my texts. So I, like, gave it a makeover. And besides, projects like this change all the time."

She was right that I'd been ignoring her, but I was still disappointed. And she was acting so weird about Shaun having bought my Con ticket — what, like it automatically meant that I owed him sex or something? And it seemed kind of soon for her to be showing off the game. It still looked pretty sloppy. I clicked through some more and bit my tongue.

"Did you see?" Lucy asked. "When you get to the end, you collect all the recipes into a cookbook called *Mastering the Art of Undead Cooking*. Isn't that funny? It's so much better this way."

"I guess," I said, gathering ammunition. "But you shouldn't have changed the whole thing around without telling me. We were supposed to be doing this together."

"Please," Lucy said, "you've barely even helped me since you started dating Shaun."

"Because you were out of town!" I said, exasperated. "How was I supposed to help you when you were all the way in Richmond Hill?"

"There are buses, you know," Lucy said. "Or how else did you and Shaun keep hanging out?"

She was right, of course, but it wasn't as if she'd even invited me up to her aunt's house. Was I supposed to read her mind?

"I have a boyfriend, okay?" I said, still mad that I had to defend myself. "It's normal to be in, like, a love bubble for a little while."

"So stay in your bubble then," Lucy said. "Just don't expect me to be there when it pops."

"Whatever," I said, "enjoy your game."

"Thanks," Lucy said, the word hung with icicles. "I will."

I walked myself out as Lucy turned back to the monitor. Her mom was in the living room as I came downstairs, and she looked confused to see me leaving so soon after I'd arrived.

"Everything all right, Victoria?" she asked.

"Fine," I said. "It's nothing."

# Thirteen

And then Mom came home. She took a cab from the airport right to Gran's, leaving her bandmates to ferry the gear back to their rehearsal space, which she swore was no big deal but which I'm sure annoyed the hell out of them. She rang the doorbell about a dozen times before I made it down the stairs to answer it, and before I'd even opened the door all the way, she'd somehow knocked me to the ground in what was probably the Guinness record for World's Biggest Hug/Wrestling Hold.

"Hey, Mom," I said, with the tiny amount of air left in my lungs from her industrial-strength embrace. "Nice to see you, too."

"Eeee! I missed you! I missed you so, so much!" she said, finally letting me up for air. "And you too, Mom." I hadn't even heard Gran sneak up behind us. Then again, Mom had had my head pinned to the floor in her finally-back-in-the-country hug/wrestling hold, so it was understandable that my hearing had been somewhat muffled. It was kind of ridiculous. Exactly how big a hug was she going to give me when she got back from being in Europe for a month and a half? Still, it felt good.

"Hi," Gran said. "It's nice to have you back. And I'm sure Victoria is ecstatic that she'll get to go home now."

"Oh, come on, Gran," I said, putting my good arm around her shoulder, "it wasn't that bad."

"Oh really?" she said. "I could have sworn that I'd interned you here against your will." She cracked a small smile. This was hands-down the closest I'd ever seen Gran come to telling a joke. Which was actually pretty cool, never mind the fact that it wasn't even remotely funny.

"Most prisoners don't get waffles," I said.

"Of course not," she volleyed, "you wouldn't want them getting fat."

I offered her a snide smile. It really wasn't like staying with Gran had been so bad, in the end. She'd mostly just let me do whatever I wanted, which was kind of ideal.

"Huh," Mom said, "when did you two become besties? You trying to give me a run for my money, Mom?"

"It's hardly fair for you to insult me just for getting along with my granddaughter," Gran said. And just as quickly as her sense of humour had appeared, it vanished back into the shadows again.

"Ah good, back to normal," Mom said. "Come on, honey, go grab your stuff. Let's go home."

"Okay," I said, "just give me a sec."

I went upstairs and jammed the last of my stuff into my backpack before I hauled it back down the stairs to say goodbye to Gran.

"It was nice having you stay with me, Victoria," Gran said, as I struggled down the last few steps.

"Yeah," I said, "it was all right. Thanks, Gran."

I went in for a hug, but Gran grabbed at the half-roll of Halls in her pocket. "My cough," she said. "I don't want to get you sick."

"Oh, come on," I said, pulling her in for a reluctant squeeze.

Mom stood by the door. "Wow," she said, "I wasn't anticipating such a Disney goodbye."

"Shut up, Mom," I said, annoyed that she wasn't allowing me to have a moment with Gran when she was the reason that I'd had to stay with her in the first place.

Gran snapped me out of the hug and scolded, "You do not talk to your mother that way."

"Okay, whatever, goodbye," I said, grabbing my backpack and dragging it through the doorway. It took another ten minutes for Mom and Gran to stop bickering long enough that Mom and I could hail a cab to take us home.

Back at the apartment we both heaved our overstuffed luggage up the stairs, only to be hit with blistering heat when we opened the door.

"I guess we better start running the AC, eh?" Mom said, locking up behind us. "This is one thing I didn't miss about being away."

"What, our apartment?" I asked, as I flopped down on the couch, my backpack abandoned by the door.

"No, dummy, I mean this sticky heat."

"Oh yeah, because everything's better in Japan, right?" I said. I was definitely trying to pick a fight, but why?

"Nooo," she said, stretching out the vowel, "but at least our hotel rooms were nice and cool. Not like this dump." She plopped herself down beside me. "How's that arm doing? About time for them to rip that cast off, isn't it?"

"Two more weeks," I said, getting up. I picked up my bag and started dragging it toward my room.

"That's it?" Mom called. "I thought I was the jet-lagged one."

"I'm just tired, that's all. I'm going to go take a nap." I started to close the door behind me.

"Fine by me," Mom said. "I could use one, too. You want to go out for dinner tonight?"

"What," I called through the closed door, "for sushi?"

"Har har. How about Hungary Thai?"

"Sure," I said, "fine."

"I missed you too, sweetheart!" she yelled loudly enough that probably half the block could hear her.

"Ugh, whatever," I said, before crashing out for some much-needed sleep in my own bed.

) ) ◗ ● ◖ ( (

A couple of hours later, Mom came knocking at my door.

"Vic, I'm starving. Let's head out."

I checked my phone. "Mom, it's, like, four-thirty, how can you be hungry for dinner?"

"My brain still thinks it's six in the morning," she said. "Let's just go, okay? I'm dying."

"You poor thing," I said, opening my door.

She was wearing a giant Hello Kitty T-shirt, and held out an identical shirt for me. "Look what I brought you!"

"You're kidding, right? You could have bought these shirts at the Dufferin Mall," I said, naming the slightly off-brand shopping mecca near our place.

"But I didn't," she said. "These are the real thing."

"You don't actually expect us to wear matching shirts to dinner, do you?"

"Oh, come on," she said. "It'll be fun! I've been away all this time — I thought you'd be into it."

Was it me trying to pick a fight, or was it her not listening to me? It pissed me off that she made me feel like it was my fault, but seriously, matching Hello Kitty T-shirts? What was I, five?

"Thanks," I said, taking the shirt from her. "But I'm not wearing it to dinner."

"Fine," she said, obviously disappointed, "have it your way. Can we just go?"

"All right. I'd hate to have you dying of starvation on my conscience."

I spent the streetcar ride over to the restaurant trying to force myself to calm down and be more patient while Mom rattled on about all the little things about Toronto that she'd missed, as if she'd been gone for years and not a couple of weeks. I told myself that it was just me being tired and she didn't mean to be so annoying. She was just trying to make up for lost time. Still, her enthusiasm for every tiny thing we saw was grating.

We ordered our usual at the restaurant, and with a glass of white wine in her hand she finally started to relax. "So it's been good for you, spending some time on your own, hasn't it?"

"Yeah," I said, eyeing a couple with heads of matching dreadlocks strolling down the sidewalk hand in hand, "actually I think it has."

"And you don't resent me too much for leaving?"

"Whatever, Mom. You're back now. It's fine."

"Yeah?" she said, taking a sip and then putting down her wine glass."You've been acting kind of weird since I got back."

"Well so have you," I said. "Why are you bouncing off the walls? Aren't you, like, super jet-lagged?"

"Yeah," she said, taking another big sip, "I am. I feel awful. Just completely run down. But you know, I wanted to come back and jump right back into things being normal."

"Uh-huh?" I said, raising an eyebrow. Well, more like raising both of them, since I've never been able to pull off that particular move.

"Okay, okay," she said holding out her hands in front of me, "I overdid it. So sue me."

"Believe me, I'm pretty sure matching Hello Kitty T-shirts count as child abuse."

"Yup, Children's Aid'll be on me in a minute, I'm sure. Which'll give you more time to spend with Shaun. How's he doing, anyway?" Damn, she was good.

"He's fine," I said, sipping at my own glass of Coke. "He's good."

"Oh really? So what'd you guys do for your birthday?"

"We, uh, saw a movie," I said.

"Oh yeah? And how did it end?" she asked, waggling her own eyebrows. Of course she could do it. She was a raised-eyebrow grand champion.

"Quit it!" I said, slapping her arm with my napkin. "We had a nice time."

"Uh huh. And …? Did he get you a present?"

"Yeah, he got me — he got us — two tickets to Fan Con next week."

"Wow," she said, "big spender!"

"Quit it. It's not like that."

"Quit what? This is great! I'm glad at least one of us is going to marry rich. I've finally got a retirement plan!"

I gave her the most withering stare I could manage.

"I'm kidding, sweets. That's great. I'm so glad you're going to get to go."

"Thank you," I said carefully, "I'm excited."

"You should be," Mom said, a little too enthusiastically. "You've got a hot date for the nerd ball!"

It was all a joke to her, wasn't it?

"Shut up," I said, "it's not like that. I mean, yeah, it's nerdy. But it's, like, cool nerdy."

"Oh no, Vic, is Shaun a nerd?" Her face fell faux-dramatically. "Does he wear taped-up glasses and have a pocket protector?" She took another big sip of wine. "Oh my god, is he a Trekkie?"

"Mom! Just quit it, okay?"

"Wow," she said, "you really like this guy, huh? You gonna have a million-dollar *Star Trek*–themed wedding? You can carry a bouquet of phasers, set to stunning!"

She laughed wildly at her own joke, and, as per usual, the other tables around us started to stare.

"I'm never telling you anything again," I said, as the waiter — the same one as always, did he never have a day off? — brought over our food.

"Aw, come on, you love me," she said, her mouth already stuffed with food. "You looove me."

"Not right now," I said, digging into my schnitzel. "You're lucky I don't turn you in to Children's Aid this second.

"You're so kind and understanding," she said. "You certainly don't get that from me."

"Uh-huh," I said, swallowing a giant mouthful of fried meat. It tasted unbelievably good. I'd missed coming here. "So what's the deal with you and the leech?"

"The leech?" Mom asked.

"This journalist guy you've been spending so much time with," I said. "What's the deal?"

"No deal. He wanted to interview me."

"Mom, I think we're about fifteen steps beyond this by now. He went to Japan with you, and you guys did weird touristy stuff together. Clearly there's something going on."

"Okay," she said, putting down her fork. "So what do you want to know?"

"Are you guys, like, dating?" I asked.

"I don't know. Maybe?" she said, draining her glass and signalling to our waiter for another one.

"Seriously?" I knew the answer before I'd even asked the question, but hearing her confirm my suspicions sank my heart like a cinder block.

"Honestly, I think you'd really like Ken. I think you will like him, once you get to know him."

"I have to meet him?" I asked.

"Well, I mean, eventually."

"So it's serious?"

"It's hard to say. It was kind of intense spending that much time together, travelling."

"What about the band?" I said. "Weren't you kind of busy rehearsing and playing shows and all that?" She was acting like she'd gone off to Japan just to be with him, like it hadn't been for the music at all.

"Of course, sweets, of course. But even still, Ken and I spent a lot of time together."

"Did you ever think that maybe he was just using you to get more material for his book?"

"Well, sure," Mom said. "I mean, that is how we met."

"And that doesn't make you just a bit, like, totally creeped out?"

"What, why creeped out?"

"He's just a fanboy, Mom!" I said, fighting to keep my voice down and losing. "How old is he even?"

"Thirty-three."

"So he's, like, five years younger than you? That's weird. That's totally weird."

"No," Mom said, accepting her second glass of wine from our waiter, "not really. Not when you're my age."

"Yeah, okay, but does he know you have a kid?"

"Sweets, he's writing a book about Dusty Moon. He knows a thing or two about my life."

"Oh, good," I said, "so he thinks that he already knows me."

"Listen to you. You're mad that he doesn't know you exist and you're mad that he does."

"So?" I said.

"So don't you think you're overreacting just a hair?"

I accidentally chomped down hard on my cheek as I stuffed another piece of schnitzel into my mouth and started whining.

"Oh, come on now, what'd you do?"

"It hurts," I said pathetically as I chewed and swallowed the too-large piece of meat.

"Okay," she said, "we can talk about this later. Clearly I need to take you back to emerg."

"Ha ha," I said pointedly, taking another big sip of my Coke.

"So when are you bringing Shaun over for dinner?"

"Try never," I said.

"Oookay. So you'll think about it then?"

"Whatever. Maybe."

We each finished our plates, the waiter brought the cheque and Mom paid with her probably maxed-out credit card. I thought about what would happen if I invited Shaun over for dinner. He'd be in fanboy heaven for sure, but that would be the end of it for me. He'd never see me as just V again. I'd only ever be Micky Wayne's daughter. He couldn't help it, I knew. That was just Mom's power.

How long could I keep my worlds apart, my love bubble and my mom bubble?

How long before it all came crashing down?

# Fourteen

The Con was coming up and, despite the weird pangs of guilt I felt for not going with Lucy, whom I still wasn't speaking to, I was really getting excited for my big date with Shaun. He and I had started texting each other ridiculously sappy messages, and I was finding it hard to put my phone down, like, ever, for fear that Mom would intercept one of our conversations.

*You're the coolest*, Shaun texted, *you know?*

*Gotta be to keep your hotness under control.*

*Oh yeah? When do I get to see your beautiful face again?*

*Con's tomorrow*, I texted, *think you can wait til then?*

*Nope, no way. Come over here this second.*

And then a minute later, *Just kidding. My parents have some people over right now. better just wait til tomorrow.*

And a third message: *You gonna pick me up?*

*Haha we better just meet there*, I texted him. *Not ready for you to meet my mom just yet.*

*I'm great with parents*, Shaun replied. *Just ask mine.*

*Hard to, I haven't met them either.*

*Fair enough. I guess we're both just mysterious orphans, eh?*

*Very mysterious. xx*

Mom poked her head in my doorway just as I was sending my last hopefully flirty text, and I scrambled to cover up the screen like she'd caught me looking at porn.

"How's Shaun doing?" she asked. Her sixth mom-sense was the worst.

"Fine. He's, uh, he's fine."

"Oh yeah?" she asked. "How fine?"

"Just whatever, okay? He's — he's good."

"Just good?" she asked.

"He's amazing," I said, as deadpan as I could manage. "He just bought a house in Morocco and he's asked me to help him pick out tiles."

"He's a keeper, that sugar daddy of yours."

"Obviously," I said. "Now before we catch our private jet to Casablanca, is there something I can help you with?"

"Well, it is eight o'clock," Mom said. "I thought it might be time for me to play mother and make us some dinner."

"Oh," I said, "right." I'd hardly noticed how hungry I was since our apartment was still so overheated, but the mention of a meal made my stomach roar.

"Great," she said, "I'm making Kraft Dinner with hot dogs, and I need you to sous-chef the dogs for me."

"You mean chop them up?" I asked, nonplussed.

"Bingo. Come keep me company while the water boils."

A pot of KD for dinner meant that Mom was totally post-tour broke. It wasn't a surprise, but it made me feel bad that we'd gone out for dinner the night before. It was just poor planning. It wasn't all bad, though, since Mom and I were serious mac-and-cheese fiends. Even the cheapest of the cheap stuff was still satisfying. Plus Mom pulled her favourite hack on the standard box and mixed cream cheese with the noodles and cheese powder and it came out surprisingly good: thick and creamy.

After we'd piled our dirty dishes in the sink, I locked myself in my room to try to pick out a perfect outfit for the next day. The Con. My big awesome date.

Mom kept yelling through the door to try to distract me from the task at hand, but it didn't work.

"You wanna watch a movie with me?" she called.

"No," I said, rejecting the third T-shirt I'd tried on, "not right now."

"You wanna go for a walk? It's such a nice night."

"It's too hot out," I said, "and anyway, I'm busy."

"What are you doing, sweets?"

I'd just rejected the fourth shirt in a row. They were all dirty, there was no time for a run to the laundromat between now and tomorrow, but I was trying in vain to pick something that made me look hot, cool, fun, and sexy and that didn't have nasty pit stains. It was basically an impossible task.

"Nothing," I called back. "Just, you know, getting ready for tomorrow."

"What's tomorrow? What's tomorrow?" she sang excitedly. Clearly the little-kid dinner we'd eaten had gone to her head.

"I told you," I said, "tomorrow's the convention."

"Oh, that's easy," Mom said, "just wear your Stormtrooper outfit. Problem solved!"

"Mom!"

"Oh right," she said, "too hot, I forgot. Maybe just your Wookiee suit."

I opened the door to yell at her properly. "This is exactly why I didn't ask for your advice. Okay?"

"Aw, come on," she said, rushing over. "Let me help. You can borrow something of mine to wear!"

"Your stuff's too small for me," I said. "What, am I going to wear your old maternity clothes?"

"Nah, I pretty much just wore extra-extra-large band shirts while I was pregnant."

"Remind me again why I'm taking fashion advice from you?"

"Because you love me," she said, before disappearing into her room. She emerged a few minutes later brandishing a yellow dress with white flowers all over it.

"It's not going to fit," I insisted. "And anyway, it's too girly."

"No, no, no," Mom said, "I think it'll work, just try it!"

I knew she wasn't going to give up, so I snatched the dress from her and shut myself in my room to try it on.

"Where did you even get this?" I asked. "How come I've never seen it before?"

"Mel's roommate had a clothing swap ages ago. I guess I just forgot I had it. I think I meant to wear it myself, but it didn't fit me quite right."

"Yeah," I said, clumsily sliding the dress over my head, "'cause you're not a fatty like me."

"Don't even," she called back. "I just wish I had your boobs. You and Gran, you guys got the good genes."

I fumbled with the zipper in the back, but it was pointless to try with my cast still on. "Can you come in and zip me up?" I asked.

"Yeah? I can come in? Does it fit?" Mom asked, barrelling into the room. Seriously. My mom is the only person in the world who barrels anywhere.

"Can you just zip?" I asked.

"Sure," she said, "one sec."

The dress tightened around me as she slid the zipper up, but miraculously the fabric seemed to hold me in just fine.

"Oh wow," Mom said, stepping around to check me out. "Take a look."

I examined myself in the full-length mirror hanging by my closet. "Yeah," I said. "It's not bad. But it's also way too fancy for the convention."

"Aw, you can dress it down," she said. "Throw on a pair of sneakers and you're good to go."

"You think?" I said, turning to scope myself out from all sides. The colour worked surprisingly well, and I had to admit that I looked pretty damn good.

"Definitely," she said. "Shaun won't be able to resist you." She smiled sagely, and then started shaking her head. "Oh, wait, no, we need to frump you up a bit. Do we have a spare potato sack anywhere? Maybe some dirt we can rub on your face?"

"Out!" I said, pointing to the door. "Thanks for the dress. On your way now."

"Aw, you're no fun," she said.

"I'm serious. We're done here."

"Okaaay. Don't stay up too late checking yourself out in the mirror!"

"I hate you," I said, closing the door behind her.

"You need your beauty sleep!"

"Good night." I called, before I collapsed on the bed. Mom was exhausting when she went on tears like this. Still, at least now I had something to wear.

Mom offered to take me to the convention centre the next morning in a fit of parental concern.

"Thanks," I said, "but I'm pretty sure I can handle the streetcar on my own."

"We could bike down together," she suggested before realizing what she'd said.

"Why don't you just put me in a baby seat on the back of your bike instead?" I asked.

"Believe me, sweets, I would if I could."

In the end she sent me off with twenty dollars, she swore we could spare it, and told me not to talk to any strange Vulcans.

I walked down to King Street and caught the street-car, and immediately noticed a couple who were for sure headed the same way I was. They were dressed up in full cosplay. It looked like they'd spent ages on their costumes, and it was kind of amazing to see them just sitting on the car, talking about nothing, while dressed as a note-perfect Mario and Princess Peach. I took a seat across the aisle from them and wanted so badly to take a picture, but I suddenly felt shy. The guts they had to be taking public transit in their costumes amazed me, and made me wish that I had that kind of nerve. Instead I contented myself with sneaking glances at them every chance I got. Princess Peach eventually noticed and blew me a cartoony kiss.

I smiled self-consciously. "You guys going to the Con?" I asked.

"How did you guess?" Peach asked, winking.

"It's-a me!" exclaimed her boyfriend, twisting his fake moustache as if on cue.

"Excuse him," she said. "He's a real method actor."

"Too bad there's no, uh, mushrooms around," I said, smiling through my weak joke.

"We came prepared." Peach pulled a couple of giant plastic red mushrooms out of her purse. These guys had really thought of everything.

"Heh, cool," I said, before turning back to my phone and leaving Peach and Mario to their conversation.

What would it take to be that confident? To not care about what anybody else thought and just let your freak flag fly? It was pretty cool, and I had to admire their nerve. I hoped I might have guts like that some-day. Mom had more guts than she knew what to do with, but maybe that kind of courageous not-caring skipped a generation. Still, I couldn't help but imagine Shaun and me dressing up next year as Stara Shah and her demigod love-interest from *LoA V:* Arcas, son of Zeus. It was a long way away I knew, in more ways than one. Still, it was nice to think about. Especially when I pictured Shaun, shirtless in a toga. If I started now, I might be able to get the outfits ready by next Con.

A little while later, when the streetcar pulled up to John Street, the costumed couple got off, and I followed them. They clearly had a better idea of where they were going than I did. I walked behind them at a distance, watching the crowds of people in costumes and superhero T-shirts multiply as we got closer and closer to the convention centre and the crowds on the street got thicker and thicker. There were lots of classic comic characters, a handful of Disney princesses, the entire cast of *Game of Thrones* and even a Lego Darth Vader. I figured that maybe I wasn't too dressed up after all, but that if someone asked me who I was I'd have to invent an obscure Swedish TV show and claim that I was in costume.

Shaun and I had been texting back and forth to try to meet up, but the crowd got more intense and packed in as I nudged closer and closer to Front Street and the convention's entrance.

*You here?* Shaun texted me.

*Yeah*, I replied, *you?*

*Uh huh. By the hot dog stand.*

*Which one?*

There were six hot dog stands around me and even more food trucks lined up along the street selling burgers, fries, and poutine.

*The yellow one*, Shaun texted.

This only narrowed it down by three.

*The yellow one with the dancing hot dog?* I replied.

*The one with the red striped umbrella*

Fifteen minutes of hot-dog-truck tag later, we finally found each other.

"Hey," he said, pulling me in for an amazing hug and then twirling me around as he let me go. "You look great."

"Thanks," I said, smoothing down the bottom of my dress. "It was this or my Stormtrooper suit."

But when I finally had a chance to take Shaun in properly, my heart sank. He was wearing a super-faded vintage band T that made his arms look amazing. The only problem? The band was Dusty Moon.

"What are you dressed up as," I asked, "a washed-up grunge kid?"

"Aw, come on," he said. "This is a great shirt. I bought it on Ebay!" He looked so proud of himself, and I realized that he might kill me if he ever found out that we have a whole box of old Dusty Moon shirts in our apartment collecting dust.

"You definitely nailed the look," I said. "Seriously, though, the costumes here are amazing. You should've seen the awesome Mario and Princess Peach I rode with on the streetcar over."

"Oh man, I wish I had," he said. "That's great. You and I should have gone as Han Solo and Princess Leia."

"Oh yeah?" I said.

"Yeah, definitely," said Shaun. "You'd look great in one of those metal bikinis."

I gave him a flirty *oh-really* smile. "Right," I said, "dream on."

"Can't blame a guy for trying."

"Uh-huh," I said, offering him my finest unimpressed stare.

"So," he said, "should we go check things out?"

"Yeah," I said, nervously eyeing the size of the crowd. "Let's go."

After wading through a line of ticket holders, we finally made it down to the convention floor. I kept almost losing Shaun to the crush of eager fans because there was so much to see. I could hardly believe how many people, and how much unselfconscious glee there was, all under one giant roof.

Shaun led me to an area called the Artist Alley and we finally stopped in front of a table where two young guys were signing copies of their comic book, the cover of which was blown up as a huge poster behind them. SAND MUMMY.

"What's up?" I asked, trying to figure out why Shaun had chosen this particular stand to pause his marathon walk through the hall.

"Heh, sorry," he said, taking off his backpack and unzipping it. He already had a bunch of comics lined up inside, and he rifled through until he found the one he was looking for. "These guys, their comic is amazing. It's hilarious. I picked up the first issue a while ago and was hoping they'd sign it. I figured I'd pick up their new issue while we were here, too."

"You came prepared," I said, checking out the contents of his backpack.

"Yeah," he said, "I've been coming here a while. My mom used to take me when I was younger. She's a big *Doctor Who* fan, and I've always been into comics."

"Isn't she bummed that you've ditched her?" I asked.

"She's got Miles. That's what younger brothers are for."

"Wow," I said, "so your whole family are hardcore Con-ers, eh?"

"Yeah," he said, giving me a sheepish smile, "kinda. You're, like, totally going to ditch me here for someone cooler, aren't you?"

"Nah," I said, "you're pretty cute. Think I'll stick around."

"Good thing I'm such a babe, eh?" he said, smiling down at the copy of *Sand Mummy #1* in his hand. "I'll just be a minute."

Shaun waited in line to get his comic signed while I hung back and scoped out another artist at a table nearby. When he came back to join me he was thrilled to show off the creators' signatures scribbled on the cover.

"Isn't this awesome?" he said. "What do you want to do next?"

"I don't know," I said, spinning around to survey the floor, overwhelmed and excited by everything I saw.

"Want to check out the exhibitor floor?" Shaun asked. "There's always lots of cool stuff there."

"Sure," I said, and let Shaun lead the way.

Passing through the double doors that led to the exhibitor floor, there were rows and rows of elaborate corporate set-ups. And that's when I saw it. What I'd forgotten I'd even been looking for.

"There," I said, pointing at the giant banner where Stara's intense gaze stared back at us.

LORE OF AGES VI: CON-EXCLUSIVE PREVIEW

"Take me."

The line-up for the *LoA VI* demo was long, but Shaun was happy to wait with me. I was so excited to see what the new game looked like, even if I hadn't quite beaten *LoA V* yet. I kept thinking that we might run into Lucy in line, and kept imagining that I saw her, but it always turned out to be someone else. Lucy was nowhere around. She'd probably been by the booth already; in fact I was almost sure she had. No way could she resist the siren song of the Con's greatest treasure.

When my turn came up, I grabbed the controller with my left hand and started running around just to see what the controls and the graphics were like. There wasn't much else I could do with only one hand but it was amazing just the same. Like a next-level version of *LoA V*, which, I realized as soon as I thought of it, was of course the point. Shaun just stood by watching me play, quietly mesmerized.

"Wow," he said, "you're really into this, huh?"

"Kind of," I said. "I mean, I love it but I'm not very good. My friend Lucy and I were actually working on making our own game for a while, but it kind of ended badly."

"What, like this?" Shaun asked.

"Ha, no," I said, "not quite. Just something really basic. It was fun."

"Yeah?" Shaun said. "That sounds cool. So what happened?"

"We had a fight," I said. "But I feel like I should kind of just apologize, you know?" The truth of my words hit me as I said them. "I've been kind of a crappy friend."

"It happens," Shaun said. "I'm sure she'll forgive you."

"Yeah, maybe," I said, as one of the staff tapped me on the shoulder and told me my time was up. "I hope so."

We spent the rest of the afternoon wandering from room to room and table to table, from fandom to fandom, losing ourselves in the crowd and the fun of it all. I got Shaun to take my picture with an amazing Stara Shah, and I took his with a guy in a rubber Batman suit who was waving a Canadian flag and calling himself Toronto Batman.

I was so overwhelmed by all the stuff for sale that I almost couldn't make up my mind on anything. In the end I was swayed by a girl selling dresses with prints of classic video games when I realized that I'd been living a shadow of a life without a *Ms. Pac-Man* dress. I had to hit an ATM and take money out just to pay for it. I knew that I'd have to lie to Mom and tell her it had been on sale for twenty bucks, but it was so worth it.

As the girl handed me my way-overpriced dress in a plastic bag, Shaun shook his head.

"You've gotta stop being my dream girl," he said. "Seriously."

"What can I say?" I said, slipping the bag into his backpack. "A dream girl's work is never done."

204

We were getting ready to leave — we'd both spent almost all of our money and only had enough left to eat at the hot dog stands outside — when I heard a just-barely familiar voice call my name.

"Vic? Hey, Vic!"

I turned around. It was Mom's friend with the purple hair from the record store. She had ditched her record-store clerk uniform of dark jeans and a band T and was dressed in a flannel shirt and jean shorts with a *Star Trek* insignia pinned to her chest.

"Hey," I said, "how's it going?"

"Good," she said, "did you guys just get here?" She stuck out her hand to Shaun. "Have we met? I'm JJ. I'm a friend of Vic's mom, Micky."

"Yeah," Shaun said, "maybe at Rotate?"

And as their hand connected, JJ noticed his Dusty Moon T. "Nice shirt," she said.

But JJ's knowing smile was totally lost on Shaun, thank God, who just shook her hand and smiled back. Was one of Mom's stupid friends going to blow my cover? I could have killed her.

"Oh," Shaun said, "cool. Thanks."

"We were just leaving," I added. "We're starving."

"Well it was great running into you! I'll see you guys around."

"Yeah," I said, "maybe."

"Your mom has cool friends," Shaun said as we crawled our way back out of the convention centre. "What label did you say she worked for again?"

"Uh, Toreador Records," I said, naming the big indie

label that had signed Dusty Moon so many years ago, and then immediately regretting it.

"Whoa, seriously?" Shaun said. "That's awesome. But aren't they, like, American?"

"Yeah," I said, "but she, you know, does stuff with their Canadian bands. And, like, with the market here. You know." I shrugged like I was sick of talking about my mom's cool job, hoping he wouldn't ask any more questions I didn't know how to answer.

Thankfully Shaun just nodded.

We finally emerged from the long line of escalators back into the daylight. "Come on." I felt around in my pocket for change and felt a stash of loonies. "I'm buying."

"A hot dog from my dream girl?" he said, clutching his chest and batting his surprisingly luscious lashes. "Be still my heart."

# Fifteen

**M**y Con date with Shaun sent my brain off into the clouds, but I couldn't put off apologizing to Lucy any longer. Shaun's parents had unceremoniously whisked him and Miles off for a weekend at a family friend's cottage — despite Shaun's protests, since we'd planned to go down to the water together after I told him about my favourite spot up on the lifeguard stands — and the *LoA VI* demo at the convention had made me homesick for the afternoons Lucy and I had spent together in front of my computer.

I knew that I'd already let things go long enough that a text-message apology wouldn't work. Sure, it sucked that Lucy had changed the game around on me, but I had to admit that *Castle Forkenstein* was pretty good, and that she'd worked really hard on it. I'd ignored Lucy, so it wasn't that surprising that she'd kept on working without me. The game was important to Lucy and I had trashed it, pretending that it was justified. It was time to grovel, but I had to do it properly. In person.

I took Mom's shopping list off the fridge (Perrier, tuna, gum, Diet Coke — as if this constituted a balanced diet) and told her I was headed out, walking as slowly as I could manage toward Lucy's parents' store. What exactly was I going to say? I swallowed my anxiety and opened the door, a little chime above me ringing as I did.

"Hi, Victoria," said Lucy's mom. "Nice to see you."

"Yeah," I said, "you, too."

I scanned the small aisles of the store, but couldn't see any sign of Lucy. Both disappointed and relieved, I quickly picked up the things that I needed from the shelves, taking a jumbo sour key with me as a snack for the walk home. I was just about to drag out my haul when the front door chime rang again and Lucy came in with her dad, mid-conversation.

"Look, I told you —" Lucy was saying to her dad, stopping short as she realized who the customer waiting to leave was.

"Lucy, Victoria's here," said her mom.

"Yeah," Lucy said, sounding supremely unimpressed, "I can see that."

"Can I, uh, talk to you for a second?"

"Go ahead," said Lucy.

"Like, outside?" I said to clarify.

"You girls go," said Lynn. "We're fine here. Just be back to help me close up, okay, Lucy?"

"Trust me," Lucy said, "I won't be gone long."

"Look," I said, when we were out of the store and earshot of her parents, "I'm really sorry. About the game, okay? I was a jerk."

"Yeah," she said, "and?"

"And I'm sorry I ignored you for Shaun," I said, putting my bag of groceries down on the pavement beside me.

"Yeah," she said, barely nodding in agreement. "And?"

"And what?" I said, "I should have come up to visit you. I shouldn't have ignored your texts. I shouldn't have ignored the game."

"Yeah," she said, "and you shouldn't have said it was cheesy when I made it better."

"Without my input," I said.

"Yeah," she said, "without you."

I gave her an unimpressed look.

"I should've told you I was working on it," she said.

"Uh-huh."

"I guess I was trying to, like, get back at you or something."

"Well yeah," I said. "And it worked."

"So are we cool? Are you going to start answering my texts again?"

"Are you going to keep sending them?" I asked.

"Depends. Think you're ready to come with me to She Shoots?"

"Wow," I said, "you're really gonna go talk about the game?"

"That's the plan," Lucy said. "They loved *Castle Forkenstein*. They invited me to come speak at the social. Tomorrow."

"You're kidding," I said, my mind officially blown.

"No," she said, "seriously. And I'm so freaked. You have to help. Will you come and present the game with me?"

"But it's your game," I said, and I meant it, though not in the way I had before.

"It was our idea," Lucy said. "Please?"

"I mean … sure," I said. "Of course. Come over and we'll figure out a plan."

"Okay," Lucy said, grabbing one of the handles of my shopping bag as I grabbed the other. "Let's go."

Back at our apartment, Lucy and I planned out how we were going to talk about *Castle Forkenstein* in front of a whole group of people. People who were probably way more experienced game-makers than we were. Who were older and cooler and, like, everything-er than us.

"Are there going to be, you know, a lot of people there?" I asked.

"Sasha said that there might be a pretty good crowd, yeah, but that everyone was, like, really supportive."

"Sasha?"

"One of the organizers," Lucy said. "Don't worry, she's nice."

"So what are we supposed to say?"

"She said just to talk a bit about how we made it," Lucy said, "and, like, what it's about and stuff. They won't be able to play the game, but I sent Sasha a screenshot and they're going to project it behind us while we talk."

"Okay," I said, letting it sink in. "Wow. This is really happening, huh?"

"Yeah," Lucy said. "It really is."

We practised talking about the game like we were presenting in front of a big group, and ran through it six times before we decided it was good enough. Or, anyway, that it was as good as it was going to get.

After that Lucy and I compared notes on the Con demo of *Lore of Ages VI*. I was right, she'd already played it twice by the time Shaun and I got there on Saturday. Talking about the new game with her got me so excited that I could hardly wait to get my cast off and get back to playing. It was hard to believe I'd had it on for almost the whole summer. It was going to be weird having two good hands again.

Making up with Lucy felt good, like a massive weight was gone from my shoulders, and geeking out with her over *LoA VI* got me feeling brave. Brave enough that I finally dug out my sketchbook to show her my imperfect drawing of Stara.

"Whoa," she said, "you did this? You should totally post it."

"Yeah? I mean, it's not done. I'm not going to be able to finish it until after I get my cast off."

"Sure," she said, "like, whenever it's ready. I didn't even know you could draw — why didn't you say something?"

"I don't know," I said. And, really, seeing Lucy's reaction, I didn't.

"So obviously you're illustrating our next game, right?"

"Yeah," I said, "obviously."

Eventually Lucy went back to the store to help close, and I went into the kitchen to help Mom with dinner. We were having beans and rice, which, she said, was what we'd be eating for the next year if I kept up my new habit of buying expensive dresses. She'd seen right through my lie that the *Ms. Pac-Man* dress had only cost twenty bucks, and was annoyed that I'd blown so much of my money when we were in kind of a tight spot.

"Next summer," she said, "you're getting a job, all right? I don't care where. I mean, as long as it's not on a pole."

We ate our meagre meal in a huffy near-silence.

The next day Mom tried to make nice. She wanted me to spend the day with her, to go for a walk or go window shopping. Something cheap. But Lucy and I were headed to She Shoots, and I still wasn't ready to tell Mom about this new part of my life. I knew that she'd wind up making some dumb joke about it all, and I wanted this to just be mine for as long as I could.

"I told Lucy that I'd spend the day with her," I said, which wasn't technically a lie.

"She could come with us!" Mom insisted.

"Sorry," I said, "under-thirties only."

"Fine, fine, fine," she said. "I should probably give Sal a call anyway. He was bugging me to come in for a late shift tonight."

"I thought we'd just have rice and beans every night until I graduated."

"If you're lucky," she said. "Pretty soon it'll be just rice. Have you seen the rising cost of beans?"

"Oh," I said, humouring her, "they're hot?"

"They're practically jumping."

"That's terrible. Even for you."

"Thank you. Thank you," she said, offering me a little bow. "You're too kind."

"I'm gonna go now," I said, "all right?"

"Okay," she said. "I'll be home late. Don't wait up."

"All right."

"Love you," she said, ruffling my hair.

"Whatever," I said, giving her a hug. "See you."

I met up with Lucy in front of her parents' store and we walked over to the address that Sasha had given her.

"Are you nervous?" I asked.

"Of course not," she said, with fake bravado. "Why, are you?"

"No way," I said, faking along with her. "I do this kind of thing all the time."

We got to the space a little before four and it was already filling up. Two dozen or so people, women and men, were milling around the room and chatting in small groups. Some wore big plastic-framed glasses and others had short, asymmetrical haircuts. A few of them were wearing band shirts, but others wore bright vintage dresses or standard-issue black jeans and T-shirts. Some were pierced, a few were tattooed, and one woman standing at the front had a hot pink streak running through her hair. A couple of women were setting up laptops and other gear at the front of the room, and Lucy and I drifted around taking it all in. It was a big, airy room that looked kind of like a space-age art-school cafeteria, but I felt like everyone was staring at us. Apart from a baby in a sling, we were the youngest people in the room by about ten years.

"This is … cool," Lucy said. "But I guess we better find Sasha?"

Though the second part was unnecessary. Just as Lucy finished saying her name, a woman with fire-engine red hair swooped in and stuck out her hand to us.

"Hi," she said, "you must be Lucy. I'm Sasha. We're so excited to have you here."

"Oh," Lucy said, having apparently lost all of her words, "yeah. Thanks."

"I'm Sasha," Sasha said again, shaking my hand. Her grip was solid. Mom would've been impressed.

"Victoria," I said. "I, uh, helped Lucy a little bit. With the game."

"Fantastic," she said, "I can't wait to hear more about it. I told a few of our members about you guys, and everyone's really excited you're here."

So that was why people were staring. Still, it was nice to be noteworthy for something other than being Micky Wayne's daughter. For the moment, anyway.

Sasha explained that we'd be hearing members of the She Shoots community talk about the projects they'd been working on during the game jam the weekend before. She said that there would be ten short presentations in all, and that we were going to be the fifth ones up. Some of the projects, she explained, would be finished games, but many of them would still be works-in-progress, and she encouraged us to talk to anyone whose work we were interested in hearing more about.

"Because trust me," she said, "everyone is going to want to talk to you."

My stomach tightened. Was I ready for this? Did messing around in Twine with Lucy make me someone worth talking to, or would all of these people be disappointed when they heard me open my mouth? My mood flipped when things finally got started, though. A woman with curly naturally red hair cut super short on one side and long on the other got up and started talking about a game that she and a friend had worked on during the jam. The game was called *Pizza Blaster*, and it looked a lot like *Space Invaders* except you played as a slice of pizza shooting at toppings and dodging the fire of rogue ranch dipping sauce.

"Huh," Lucy whispered to me, "cool."

"Yeah," I said, nodding, "totally."

There were three more presentations after that, and I was amazed at how many different kinds of stories were being told and how many ways there were to design games. One was a Twine game designed to show what it felt like to have an eating disorder, and another was about the origins of food and came complete with retro-style pixel art.

There was a big round of applause as the *Organic Trail* group finished, and then Lucy and I were up.

"Here goes nothing," Lucy whispered to me as Sasha called us up to the front.

"You'll be great," I whispered back. "Trust me."

Standing at the front of the room, I realized that the crowd was even bigger than it had been when we arrived. Smiling faces filled the space, and glancing to the side I saw the screenshot of *Castle Forkenstein* projected next to us.

Suddenly all the blood in my body rushed up to my head and I felt high. I felt strong. This was awesome.

Beside me, Lucy took a big breath and started her speech, just like we'd planned. She talked twice as quickly as she had when we rehearsed, and I stumbled over my words a few times and had to pause for encouragement, but we were done before I knew it, and then the room filled up to the ceiling with applause.

I felt lightheaded as we walked back and took our seats in the crowd. Strangers on all sides of us smiled and nodded, high-fived us, and whispered, "Nice job!" before the next group got up to present their game.

"You good?" I whispered to Lucy.

"Oh yeah," she whispered back, "real good."

Lucy and I were mobbed when the presentations ended, and we answered questions about how long we'd been using Twine, what else we were planning to do with the game and what projects we wanted to work on next. I gave Lucy all the credit to anyone who asked, but she insisted that I was the brain behind the castle, and that I would be illustrating whatever our next project was.

"That was great!" Sasha said, coming over to us as the crowd slowly wandered off. "Did you guys have fun? I'd love to talk to you both some more about —" she broke off, recognizing a familiar face that was just behind us. "Hey, Ken! How's it going?"

I turned around. The guy behind me was almost six inches shorter than I was, and wearing a faded Black Flag shirt. There were grey hairs sprinkled through his other- wise black hair, with a pair of Wayfarer sunglasses perched on top. This guy was named Ken. But it couldn't be …

"Good," he said, "nice to see you. Sorry I missed the big show."

"That's all right," she said, "you working late?"

"Yeah, I've got so much transcribing to do. I'm way behind on my deadline on the …" he paused and turned to me. "Hey, we haven't actually met yet, have we? It's Vic, right?"

Oh no.

"No," I said, "who are you?"

"I'm Ken. I'm — well, I'm a friend of your mom's."

*Oh no.*

"You know Victoria?" Sasha asked, "She and Lucy here just gave a great presentation about a game they've been working on in Twine.

"Yeah?" Ken said, "Wow, that's awesome. Your mom didn't mention that you, well …"

"Just one second, all right?" Sasha said, inter- rupting the awkward pause. "I'm so sorry, but there's someone else here I have to talk to for a second. I'll be right back, though, okay?"

And, as cool as Sasha was, in that moment I could have killed her with my bare hands.

"So," Ken said, trying to break the uncomfortable silence that was mounting around us, "you guys made a game?"

"Yeah," I said, offering him nothing to work with.

"Yeah," said Lucy, catching the vibe immediately.

"Cool. Cool. I'm —" Ken said. He was sweating. "I really like your mom, you know. She's a great, you know, interview subject." I could tell that he immediately regretted his choice of words, but there was no way I was going to help him out of this mess.

"That's all she is to you?"

"Of course not. That came out wrong."

"I bet. What are you even doing here?"

"I'm a friend of Sasha's. I work here sometimes. Out of this space, I mean. When I'm writing. It's a shared working space — I spend a lot of time here."

Great, so there was no way that I could get rid of him.

"Yeah," I said, "whatever. Anyway, we've gotta go."

"Okay, cool," he said, smoothing back his hair that wasn't long enough to be smoothed. "Well, it was great to meet you. Tell your mom I said hey."

"Hey?" I said incredulously.

"Yeah. I mean, if you want to."

"Fine," I said. "Let's go, Luce."

And as disappointed as I'm sure Lucy was to not stick around and talk more to Sasha and the other members of She Shoots, I was grateful that she followed me without a word as we power-walked out of the place and headed back toward home.

We didn't talk much. We were just trying to process everything that we'd seen. Our first-ever taste of being, well, popular. People wanted to meet us and help us and work with us. Who cared if Lucy's *LoA* friends didn't like me — here was a whole room full of people excited to meet me just because I was there. It was hard to believe how good it felt.

On the other hand, there was Ken. He seemed okay in a dorky Mom's-boyfriend kind of way. I hated to admit, but he was pretty good-looking and clearly indie-game-maker-approved cool, but there was no way that I could make the group something all my own if he was constantly going to be on the periphery.

"So," I said when we finally stopped in front of Lucy's house, "that was something."

"Yeah," she said. "No kidding."

"Back to work tomorrow?" I asked.

"We don't want to disappoint our fans."

# Sixteen

Finally the day I'd scheduled to have my cast taken off arrived. Mom and I went back to the hospital, and, after checking that my arm had healed up all right, they took this weird little saw and cut it off.

It felt strange to see my right wrist again as they peeled the cast away. I held my arms up next to each other, and the left one made me look like a tanning-bed addict compared to how pasty white the right one was. I even had a tan line around where the cast had been, like a farmer's tan, only ten times worse.

"Hahaha, whoa! Bet you didn't think of that, huh, sweets?" Mom said as I noticed how brutal my tan line was. "Maybe if you ask nicely they'll put it back on for you."

I tightened my hand into a fist and then stretched out my fingers. It was so amazing just to move my hand again that I could almost tune out her terrible joke.

"Guess it's about time we got your bike fixed up, eh?"

I rotated my hand around slowly to test my wrist, it was still pretty tender. "Yeah, soon," I said. I missed

PYT but I had to admit that the idea of getting back on my bike still spooked me. "I don't think I'm ready just yet."

"Guess it's about time I bought a minivan to drive you around in then," she said.

"Oh sure," I said. "And knowing you, it'll be a VW van that smells like some hippie dude's armpit."

"Sounds great," she said, "sign me up."

From the hospital, Mom had to rush off to band practice. The big Island show was happening the next day and the band had been kind of slacking off since they'd gotten home from Japan.

"I was thinking we'd have dinner together tonight," Mom said.

"Yeah," I said, "that's what we usually do."

"No," Mom said, "but I mean you and me and ... well, I want you to meet Ken."

She didn't know, of course, that I'd already met him. I didn't know how to explain our run-in without telling her all about She Shoots and our game, too, and I'd been putting that off as long as I could. Tonight was going to be the end of all that. I felt instantly depressed.

"I think you're really going to like him," she said. But I didn't buy it.

"I doubt it," I said, my mouth a perfect flat line. A dead heartbeat.

"I know it's not convenient that I fell for him," Mom said, scanning for a streetcar to take her south to the Rehearsal Factory. "It's terrible timing. And it's weird for sure that we met because he's writing this book, but that's just the way it happened. I really like this guy. And I think you will, too."

"He's seriously coming for dinner tonight?" I asked.

"I invited him and he said yes," Mom said, still barely looking at me. "Why don't you invite Shaun over, too?"

I thought back to Shaun's Dusty Moon shirt, to the fact that I'd finally gotten comfortable being my real self around him. No way was I going to let Mom get in the way of that, to let the fact that I was Micky Wayne's daughter override everything that Shaun and I had already shared. She was already going to find out everything about She Shoots from Ken. Shouldn't I get to keep at least one secret? The lie came out fully formed before I'd even had a chance to think about it.

"We're breaking up," I said. "I'm dumping him. Tomorrow. It's not working out."

"Oh, I'm so sorry, sweets. I know you really liked him," she said, pulling me in tight for a hug. And for the first time in six weeks I was able to give her a real one back, though I didn't feel like it.

"Yeah," I said, "so maybe it could be just us for dinner tonight? I'm feeling kind of, you know, fragile."

"Uh-huh," Mom said, "sure, it can absolutely be just us for dinner."

Her streetcar was just pulling up in front of us and she was checking to make sure she had enough change.

It was childish, I knew, but I just wasn't ready to have the leech in our apartment. To have him prowling through our stuff, looking for weird tidbits to make his book even juicier. As if the rumour that Dennis was alive and well in Mexico wasn't enough.

"Look, sweets, I have to go," Mom said. "We'll talk more about this Shaun stuff when I get home, okay?"

She climbed the steps to the streetcar, and, just as it pulled off, she yelled out one of the barely cracked windows, "Can you make dinner?"

I spent the rest of the afternoon hanging out at home. Our ancient air conditioner had finally kicked the bucket, but fortunately since it was the end of August the heat had dulled just enough that it wasn't totally suffocating.

I painted my nails highlighter yellow, but then messed them up and had to start all over. It felt so good to have two hands again. Everything was so much better. How had I taken an entire hand for granted for so long?

I pulled out my phone and texted Shaun. Right-handed, what a luxury.

*Whats up, big boy?*

*Nothing*, he replied a few minutes later. *Just wishing you were here.*

*Oh yeah?*

*Oh yeah.*

*Sooo*, I texted, *I got my cast off today …*

*Oh really??* His reply was almost instantaneous.

*Yup.*

*Does your arm feel weird?*

*Yeah*, I texted, *kinda. But it's awesome to have the cast off.*

*Yeah I bet*, he texted.

Then a second message: *Oh! I almost forgot!*

And a third: *I won us 2 tickets to that big show on the Island tomorrow. Micky Wayne is playing! You know, from Dusty Moon!*

If I'd felt depressed before, this was my rock bottom. I was keeping Mom and Shaun separate, in different compartments of my life, for their own good. Why were they both trying so hard to ruin everything?

I couldn't turn down a sweet date like that with Shaun, but there was no way I could avoid him figuring out who my mom was if we went together. But it was also Mom's biggest show of the summer, the biggest in-town show she'd had in ages, and she'd be crushed if I didn't go.

There was basically no way I could make it work. I couldn't avoid going to the Island, and I wanted to go with Shaun. Maybe, I thought desperately, I could convince him to hang out far away from the stage with me, and then just tell Mom that Lucy and I wanted the full crowd experience instead of watching from backstage like we usually did. Mom would be hurt, I knew, but she'd forgive me. And then I'd just have to get Lucy to pretend that she'd been with me if Mom ever asked.

Then I remembered: I really had told Lucy that we'd go to the show together, back when Mom first booked it back at the beginning of the summer. How had I forgotten? I really had been a bad friend. I was going to have to hang out with Shaun and Lucy together. The compartments of my life were seriously falling to pieces. But the three of us could find a spot in the crowd, somewhere far from the stage, somewhere Mom would never see us. It could work. As long as Lucy promised to keep quiet about who Mom was.

It was a weak plan for sure, but it was the best I had.

*Oh, cool,* I texted Shaun. *Sounds good.*

*Back to the island,* he replied. *Just like our first date.*

*Haha don't remind me.*

*Lets do it right this time.*

Was that even possible? There was no way. But I couldn't tell Shaun that.

*Oh yeah.*

Mom came home late from band practice, and since the only real food left in the fridge was eggs, half a can of beans, and the end of a jar of salsa, I made us a weak approximation of huevos rancheros. I imagined for a second what the real thing might taste like if I'd just woken up in Mexico. And if there was no one around who knew who I really was.

"You guys ready for tomorrow?" I asked as we dug into our slightly scorched meal.

"Yeah," Mom said, "I think it's going to be great. We're going to be heading out there pretty early for sound check, so you might just want to head over on your own later. Is Lucy coming with you?"

For once it was like Mom had actually read her lines.

"Yeah," I said, "we'll probably go out a bit later. And, uh, we might just, like, hang out with the main crowd. You know, not come up on stage or anything?"

"Aw, really?" she said, "I love having you up on stage with me. Gives me that extra bit of confidence before I go on, you know? You sure you guys just want to be in the crowd? There's going to be a ton of people there. You probably won't be able to see very well."

"It's fine. I think some other kids from our school are going to be there. I just want to be, you know, normal tomorrow, okay?"

"You are anything but normal, my dear," Mom said, taking a big bite of her eggs. "That's the price we both pay. Anyway, you know you can always come on stage with me. And Lucy, too. Just think about it."

"Okay," I said, her words stuck on repeat in my head. The price we both paid. Was it worth all of this?

"Oh my gosh," Mom said, interrupting her own loop, "I haven't even asked you about what happened with Shaun. I thought you guys were getting along so well. Was it something at the Fan Con? Did something happen?"

"Uh-huh, yeah," I lied. "He just kept, you know, walking ahead of me like he didn't even care that I was with him. I don't know, I guess it just wasn't as good as I thought. Like, if he doesn't care about me, whatever. I can do better."

"You sure he just wasn't really excited to be there? Did you tell him you thought he was ignoring you?"

She wasn't helping. I should've come up with a better reason, but I didn't want to paint Shaun like a total ass.

"Yeah, no, it's, like, it's a lot of things," I said. "I just don't think I want to have a boyfriend right now. It's too much."

"Is it sex?" Mom asked. "Is he making you feel like you have to —"

"Mom!" I said, dropping my fork.

"What? He's a teenage boy. You think I didn't have sex before I was ready just because my idiot boyfriend wanted to?"

"What are you talking about," I said, "you mean with Dennis?"

"No, this was Davey. My first boyfriend. I was fourteen. I wasn't ready, he was. Get it?"

"Didn't you say you were fifteen?" I asked. This wasn't exactly the wildly romantic story I remembered Mom telling me. About the beach, the sand, everything.

"I lied," she said. "That story I told you?"

I nodded. "Yeah?"

"That was my second time. I didn't have sex for six months after the first. Until after my birthday. I was surprised that Davey stuck around that long, but he did. And eventually it got better and I started to like it. That first time sucked, though. I mean, it wasn't traumatic or anything, but I wished I hadn't done it. And that's why I don't tell it."

"You were fourteen?" I asked, still hung up on this particular detail.

"Fourteen." She scooped up her last mouthful of eggs and chewed thoughtfully. "Anyway, I'm glad you've got more sense than I ever did. I always knew you were smarter than me."

"Yeah," I said, "sure."

I picked up our plates and dumped them in the sink. I ran hot water over them for a minute, but figured that

I'd leave Mom with the dirty dishes. It was the least she could do since I'd cooked.

"Oh, sweets, I know it's a pain, but I've really got to look over some of these event details for tomorrow. Would you mind cleaning up?"

"Can't we just do them tomorrow?" I asked. What was I, her maid now? I'd only just graduated from being her shadow.

"I know, but we're going to be so busy tomorrow and the salsa totally cakes on the plates. I hate when that happens. Could you? Just this once?"

And just as I was about to tell her off for passing the buck on the tiniest of household chores and therefore totally sucking at being a mom in general, something way worse came knocking.

Quite literally. Well, almost. Someone rang our doorbell at the bottom of the stairs.

Mom went down and opened it as I started reluctantly soaping up the pile of dishes in the sink. She appeared at our door a minute later, with Ken the Leech in tow.

"Hey, Vic," Ken said, taking off his shoes. "Nice to see you again."

"Again?" Mom said. "What do you mean?"

"Are you fucking kidding me?" I said to Mom, ignoring Ken's existence altogether. "I told you I didn't want him coming over tonight."

"Whoa," Ken said, "I should go." He bent down and started clumsily trying to stick his feet back into the still-tied sneakers he'd just pulled off.

"Hold it," Mom said, and then turned to me. "You don't talk to me that way. You don't talk to anyone that way, you know that."

"Yeah, and you know that I told you I wanted it to be just us tonight. I don't want him here."

"You told me that you wanted it to be just us for dinner, so I told Ken to come over afterwards," Mom said, turning to put a hand on his arm, "It's fine, Ken, you can stay. Vic's just upset because she's going through a bad breakup."

"You don't even know!" I said, my voice was so loud that it filled the room. It could have filled every room. I'd had enough. "You don't know my life anymore! And instead of trying to figure out who the hell I am without you, I have to worry about you running around with some obsessive fanboy who's just using you to write some fucking book about my dead dad!" I slammed down the glass I was holding and it smashed into a million little pieces in the sink, then I went to my room to grab my stuff.

Mom followed me and barricaded my bedroom door with her body, straining to keep her voice low and even. I figured that Ken had already bailed. Maybe a big scene was all I needed to make sure that he'd leave us alone for good.

"Where are you going?" she asked slowly, giving each word weight.

"I'm not staying here tonight. I'm going over to Lucy's. It's disgusting what you're doing. You're falling for someone who wants to squeeze you dry for your story."

Mom pinched the bridge of her nose, breathed in deeply and then back out. "I can't talk to you about this right now, you're being completely irrational. Do you know what kind of stress I'm under? You had to pull this with me tonight of all nights? I have a show tomorrow. A really important show. You know that."

"So this is all about you?" I said, stuffing my phone into my bag. "Then I'm going. Have a great show tomorrow. I'll be sure to tell all my friends what a beautiful fucking star my mother is."

"Just go to Lucy's," she said. "And text me when you get there so I know that you're okay."

"God, you're really going for Mother of the Year, huh?"

"We'll talk about this later," she said. "After tomorrow. Just give me that much."

"Fine, whatever."

I pushed past her and out the door. Mercifully, Ken had already split.

I started running as soon as I hit the street. People meandering on the sidewalks gave me weird looks as I rushed past them, heading west. With tears burning down my cheeks and my bag *thump-thumping* against my side, I looked like a mess, but I couldn't stop moving. When my legs finally ached so badly that I knew I had to stop, I straightened up to see where my feet had taken me.

Shaun's house.

# Seventeen

I went around the side of the house, where I hoped Shaun's parents or any snooping neighbours couldn't see me, and texted him.

*Outside. Let me in?*

*Outside where?* Shaun replied.

*Your place*, I texted. *Are you home?*

*Yeah, just got in. Come around the back, okay? I'll let you in. Just be quiet.*

A motion-sensing light went off as I came around the back of the house, but fortunately no one seemed to notice. Shaun's parents had a beautiful backyard, with flowers and plants sprouting in just about every direction, but somehow the peacefulness of it all was jarring after my big fight with Mom and it jumpstarted my tears again.

A minute later Shaun's face appeared at the back door.

"Hey," he whispered through the screen, "what's going on?"

Then he saw my pathetic face, and opened the door as quickly as he could without making it squeak and pulled me into a deep hug. He wrapped around me so perfectly, and with two good arms I folded myself into him completely. Eventually I stopped crying.

"It's my mom," I whispered. "I can't go home tonight."

"Okay," he said, "just be quiet. My parents are upstairs watching a movie, and they're probably asleep by now anyway. Just come up to my room, okay?"

I sniffed hard and nodded, following him upstairs as quietly as I figured was humanly possible. We paused at the top of the stairs when Shaun thought he heard a noise from his parents' room, but it turned out to just be a Jurassic snore. Shaun led me into his bedroom and closed the door behind him.

"Come here," he said, "lay down with me. What happened?"

"Just a sec," I said, pulling out my phone. As furious as I was at her, I knew Mom would ask fewer questions if I just sent her a stupid text saying I was okay. I hoped that she'd be too busy in the morning to call Lucy's parents to check in on me, but at that point I hardly cared. What was one lie on top of everything else? I just didn't want her to think that I was lying belly-up in a ditch somewhere with a needle in my arm. Not that there were any ditches downtown anyway.

Mom texted back a single word.

*Good.*

I shuddered at how quickly she'd responded, then tossed my phone to the other side of the bed where I wouldn't have to look at it.

"Can we just watch a movie?" I asked. "Something stupid? Please?"

"Yeah," he said, "of course."

"And I'm not having sex with you tonight, okay?"

"You think that's what I want when you show up at my back door, with friggin' geyser eyes?" he asked. "Come on, give me some credit."

I laughed and sniffed hard. "You're right. You're such a sensitive guy."

"Obviously," he said. "Just don't go spreading that around, all right?"

"Our secret."

He pulled out his laptop and I made it through about fifteen minutes of *Step Brothers* before passing out cold, splayed out over most of Shaun's bed.

Shaun nudged me awake at an absurdly early hour the next morning. "Come on," he whispered, "get up."

"It's okay," I whispered, my mouth still slow with sleep, "I'll get out."

"No," he said, "I meant, I'm coming with you. Let's go get breakfast."

"Yeah?" I said.

"Yeah. But we've gotta leave now, before my folks wake up."

I'd passed out wearing all of my clothes, so I was ready to go in a minute. Shaun wasn't shy at all about changing in front of me, and I found myself staring at him as he took off his boxers and put on fresh clothes. He had a mole on the small of his back and it was the most perfect little spot I'd ever seen on another person. I instinctively memorized its coordinates and its size.

Once he'd swabbed his pits with deodorant, he was ready to go. And when he turned around to face me, I saw that he was wearing his Dusty Moon shirt again.

"What?" he said, when he saw the look on my face, "too much? I know you're not supposed to wear the shirt of the band you're going to see, but isn't this a little different?"

There was no way I could tell him not to wear the shirt without ruining everything, so I just shrugged. "No, it's fine. It's a nice shirt."

"Thanks," he said. "Now we better get out of here."

We were halfway down the stairs when all of our good luck ran out. We'd been perfectly silent all the way down the hall, and I was just starting to think that we should write a manual on how to be totally stealth, when the door at the end of the hallway opened and a woman with cropped grey hair in a faded T-shirt and plaid flannel shorts stepped out.

"Hello," she said, "I don't believe we've met."

I was paralyzed. My body's impulse was to run, but I knew that wasn't an option. At least not outside of a cheesy sitcom.

"Hi," I said, holding up my hand in a static wave.

"V, just go downstairs, okay?" Shaun said. "Give me a second. Don't leave."

I could feel Shaun's mom's laser vision burning a hole through the back of my head as I walked the rest of the way downstairs and took an uneasy seat on the couch. Upstairs, a door creaked and then shut and I couldn't hear their voices anymore. I sat perfectly still with my feet flat on the floor like the whole world might crack in half if I moved.

A few anxious minutes later, when Shaun still hadn't come back downstairs, I heard a door open and then fast plodding footsteps heading toward me on the stairs. I finally turned my head just as Miles hopped up to his usual spot on the couch. He turned on the TV, picked his controller up off the coffee table, and resumed his game of *Dragonfury Infinite* without saying a word. I sat there watching him play for a few more minutes before he finally opened his mouth.

"What do you play?" he asked.

"Huh?" I said, startled by the sound of his voice.

"You play, right?" he said, not taking his eyes off the screen.

"Um, yeah," I said, "a bit. I like *Lore of Ages*."

"Yeah," he said. "The new one's gonna be sweet."

"Totally," I said, exhaling the last bit of breath I had left in my lungs before we returned to our mutual silence.

A few minutes later, I heard a door open upstairs and then three sets of footsteps made their way down the stairs. Shaun reached the bottom step first, flanked by two women: one who I'd already met, though she was now wearing jeans, and the other who had her hair in a ponytail and her mouth in a tight smile.

"Mom, Alice," Shaun said, "this is Victoria."

I stood up from the couch at the introduction. I wasn't sure if I should shake their hands or not, but figured the fact that they'd caught me sneaking out of Shaun's room first thing in the morning meant that we were probably past the pleasantries stage.

"Hi," I said. "It's, uh, nice to meet you."

"I told them why you came over last night," Shaun said, by way of explanation as to why his parents hadn't run me out of their home yet. "That you had nowhere else to go. Right?"

"Yeah," I said, trying to look as harmless and pathetic as possible. "Right."

"While we disagree with the way you and Shaun went about this," the first woman, Shaun's mom, said.

"We have always said that our home would be a safe place for anyone who needed it," said the second woman, Alice. "So, welcome."

"They want you to stay for breakfast," said Shaun. "Okay?"

"Oh, yeah, sure," I said. "Okay."

Shaun's mom got to work cracking eggs into a large cast-iron skillet, while Alice tried unsuccessfully to get Miles to set the table. Shaun took a brick of cheese from the fridge and started grating it into a painted ceramic bowl, and I stood around uselessly, unsure of how to help.

"Um, can I … is there anything I can do?" I asked.

"It's fine," said Alice, who had given in and started setting the table herself. "Just have a seat. Would you like some juice?"

"Thanks," I said, "but I'm fine."

I watched Shaun's family's choreographed chaos from my seat at the table. Shaun's mom started throwing vegetables and cheese into the skillet, and soon she was setting neatly folded omelettes onto the plates Alice had arranged on the table. Shaun took a seat next to me with a giant glass of juice in his hand.

"All right?" he whispered to me, a deep crease cutting through his forehead.

"Yeah," I said, as his parents took their seats. "Fine."

"Miles," Shaun's mom called, "put the game down. It's breakfast time."

But he didn't seem to be listening. The rest of us smiled uncomfortably at each other around the small table.

"Miles," Shaun's mom called again, "your eggs are getting cold."

"Yeah, yeah," he said, waving her off with one hand.

Shaun's mom got up from the table and stood between Miles and the TV. "Breakfast," she said. "Now."

Miles sighed loudly and put down his controller, then came over and joined us at the table. We all picked up our forks and started eating, and I was grateful for the excused silence. Miles was the first to clear his plate, which took him all of six giant bites, and soon he was back on the couch, controller in hand.

As Alice reached the middle of her omelette, she said, "So, Victoria, you and Shaun go to school together?"

"Mmhmm," I said. "I've actually been over here once before. We were rehearsing a play."

"I remember that play," Alice said. "It was … interesting. How's your summer been?"

"It's been fine, mostly," I said. "I, uh, broke my wrist back in July. So that wasn't good. But otherwise it's been okay."

"And what's going on right now with you and your mom?" she asked.

"Alice," Shaun's mom said, "it's not the time."

"Yeah," Shaun said, "just leave it, okay?"

"No," I said, "it's fine. I can talk about it. You guys are, like, really nice for not kicking me out."

"You hear that?" Alice said to Shaun's mom, "We're nice."

"She's clearly been misinformed."

I smiled. "Yeah, my mom … she's, well, we're just not getting along right now. Which isn't like us. We're, like, usually really close."

Alice nodded but didn't interrupt me, and I wondered how much I could confide in Shaun and his parents without giving my secret away.

"She's dating this guy who, like, I just don't think is good for her. And she can't see what's right in front of her face, that he's using her."

It was Shaun's mom's turn to nod.

"How do you mean?" Shaun asked.

That was a question I couldn't answer.

"He's just bad," I said, "I don't trust him. I can't go home right now. I mean, I will soon, just not today."

"That's fine," Alice said.

"But we'll ask that if you need to spend the night again that you sleep on the couch," Shaun's mom added.

"Oh yeah," I said, "of course. I'm really sorry about last night. I just, well, I was desperate."

"That's enough of the third degree for one morning," Shaun's mom said, as she finished her breakfast.

"Are you still hungry?" asked Alice. "Would you like us to make you something else?"

"No, no," I said, "I'm stuffed. That was really good. Thank you."

"She's quite a cook, isn't she?" said Alice.

"Oh, stop it," Shaun's mom said. "Now we'll go back upstairs and leave you two to clean all of this up, all right?"

"Oh yeah," I said, "sure."

"We're on it," said Shaun.

Soon Shaun was up to his elbows in sudsy water, and I was wielding a rag to dry off the wet dishes.

"Your parents are, like, so cool," I whispered. "That was so decent of them."

"Yeah," he said, "they're pretty all right most of the time."

"So, Alice …?"

"She's my step-mom," Shaun said, handing me a glass.

"Oh," I said, toweling it off, "gotcha."

"I hope it's not weird that I didn't tell you," he said.

"You didn't have to, Miles did. But, I mean, you could have, you know."

"Yeah," he said, handing me a cheese grater, "I know. I just get annoyed with feeling like I have to explain my family to people all the time. We're just us, you know?"

"Yeah," I said. And having spent only one meal with his family, that much was already perfectly clear. They were just themselves. And it was kind of amazing.

"So are we still on for the show today?" Shaun asked, pulling the plug up from the bottom of the sink and draining out the water.

"You sure you're not grounded?" I asked.

"Oh, no, I absolutely am. But my folks said we could take the day before they lock me up for the rest of my life."

"I guess we better enjoy it then."

"I think it's our duty," Shaun said. "So do you want to head down to the Island a bit early? To hang out on the beach and stuff before the show starts?"

"Yeah," I said, trying to figure out how I was going to swing meeting up with Lucy, too, "that's fine."

"Aw, come on," he said, "it's going to be great. Micky Wayne!"

I pictured it: Mom in her element with Ken watching her from backstage, scribbling in some tiny little note-book, trying to capture the impossible magic she radiated when she performed and probably getting off in the pro-cess. But I didn't want to disappoint Shaun, he'd been basically perfect to me. The faded letters of his T-shirt seemed like a flashing neon sign. DUSTY MOON. DUSTY MOON. Was he ever going to see me the same way again once he knew the truth? There was just no way.

Shaun went upstairs to tell his parents we were going, and I sent out a pair of texts.

To Lucy I texted, *Hey! Going to the beach with Shaun before the show tonight, but text me when you're heading over and we'll meet you there.*

I knew Lucy wouldn't be thrilled at this, but at least I wasn't ditching her completely.

And then I texted Mom. Two words were all I needed: *I'm alive.*

Shaun and I caught the Queen streetcar headed toward the Island ferry docks, and I shivered as we passed the spot where I'd been doored all those weeks before. It felt like forever ago. Shaun held my arm and traced the tan line where my cast had been with his index finger.

"Don't worry," he whispered into my hair. "This time we'll do it right."

And then I shivered again.

# Eighteen

After a few transit snarls, we got to the docks a little before noon. Even though the concert wasn't going to start until four or five, the crowds were already starting to swell around the ticket booths and it took us forever just to get up to the front. Shaun wasn't the only one wearing a Dusty Moon shirt, either. We spotted at least five other people wearing the same T and Shaun exchanged a knowing nod with each one of them.

"This is going to be so great!" he said, squeezing me to his side. "The whole lineup's great, but I seriously can't wait to see Micky Wayne. I hear she toured Japan this summer. Isn't that cool?"

It was going to take another fifteen minutes, tops, before Shaun put what he knew about my mom together and figured out what my big secret was. "Yeah," I said nonchalantly, "really cool."

When we finally snaked our way to the front of the line, Shaun paid for both of our tickets.

"M'lady," he said, holding one out to me.

"Oh no," I said, "no, no, no, no. We're not going down that road. No m'lady."

"Yes, m'lady," he said, as we handed over our tickets to the woman standing by the ferry gates.

The concert crowd was waiting for the boat to Centre Island, but I pointed to the line for Ward's instead.

"Don't want to go back and visit our friends at Hanlan's Point?" Shaun asked.

"Oh god," I said, hiding my face with my newly healed right hand. "Worst first date ever."

"I had fun."

"You didn't break your arm," I said, booping his nose.

"Good point."

The Centre Island ferry arrived, and the band-shirted crowd thinned out a little bit. Finally our ferry docked and Shaun and I climbed aboard with the rest of the assembled crowd. We fought our way to the front of the boat and wrapped our arms around each other. This time I didn't care how cheesy we looked, and knew that we didn't need to take any selfies to prove that we'd been here. Just staring off at the lake with the mist in our faces was perfect. I felt totally myself. And then we took a selfie anyway, just because. Then my phone died. I hadn't charged it, I realized, in a couple of days. Damn.

Eventually we docked and Shaun and I ambled our way toward the beach. We laid ourselves out in the sand, kicked off our shoes and lay there in the sun. Here, everything was beautiful. The city was a far-away vision across the lake, and even the hyper concertgoers seemed miles away; they were on a whole other island, after all. I nodded off in the sun with Shaun's faint snores in my ear.

Then, all of a sudden, we heard guitars. It sounded like fifty of them all playing at the same time and we both jolted awake.

"Oh!" Shaun said. "It's starting. I think this is Grey Matters, I hear they're really good. Should we go check it out?"

Why did we have to spoil such an amazing day by going to Mom's stupid concert?

"Let's hang out here a little while longer," I said. "I mean, Micky isn't even going on 'til, like, nine, right? It's only, what, like four o'clock now?"

Shaun checked his phone. "Oh man, it's six."

"Guess our brains have been frying pretty steadily in the sun."

"Yeah," he said, "seriously. So you and Micky Wayne are pretty good friends, eh? You on a first-name basis now?"

"Heh, yeah," I said, laughing off my mistake. "We're tight."

How much longer could I pull this off? How much longer could I keep him distracted enough not to ask questions? "Come on," I said, "let's go for a walk."

Shaun looked reluctant.

"Let's find somewhere a bit more … private, okay?" I took his hand and squeezed tight.

"Oh," he said, his eyes flashing to life. "Yeah, okay, let's go."

We ambled our way down the main road of the Island, which was really just a small paved path.

244

"I hope she plays 'Stranded in Daylight,'" Shaun said. "I mean, your good friend Micky Wayne. You think she will?"

"Stranded in Daylight" had been Dusty Moon's biggest hit, and Mom hated when people called it out when she played solo. Still, she usually wound up dredging it out for an encore because it made people lose their minds, even if was just her and her backup band covering an old song.

"Maybe," I said, "but she'll probably be mostly playing her solo stuff."

"Yeah, I like her solo stuff, too, but you can't touch those old Dusty Moon songs. They're just so good, you know?"

"Uh-huh," I said, scanning the field in front of us for a secluded spot, becoming less and less turned on by the moment. "Why don't we try to find a place over here?"

We walked off the path toward some bushes. The sun was already dipping lower in the sky, and the light was becoming a soft, warm glow. We found a tiny clearing in the middle of the brush and sat down cross-legged with our knees touching.

Shaun pulled a joint out of his pocket. "I was saving this for Micky Wayne's set, but, like, maybe we should just smoke it now."

"Yeah," I said, stretching my legs out in the grass. "Sounds good."

We passed the joint back and forth. I'd already built up a decent tolerance from smoking with Shaun that summer, and I hardly coughed at all.

"Lie down with me," I said, spreading my arms and legs out like I was making snow angels in the tall grass.

Shaun lay down on top and started kissing me. I kissed him back, hard. And suddenly we'd disappeared into a cloud of hands and arms and mouths and tongues. He tasted like smoke and salt. I pulled his shirt up over his head and planted a line of kisses from his belly-button to his neck.

He protested for half a second, acting shocked.

"Whoa," he whispered in my ear.

I unbuttoned his shorts and he slid them down to his knees.

My head was perfectly cloudy as Shaun pulled off my shirt too. He was this amazing, practically glowing, person. And I loved him. I did. I loved the mole on his back and his little bit of belly. I loved his pudgy cheeks and his high forehead. I loved his hair, freshly buzzed again, that I couldn't stop rubbing.

"I love you," I said quietly, before raising my hand to my lips, as if trying to stuff the words back in after it was already too late.

"I love you, too," he said, taking my hand away from my mouth and kissing my fingers.

How many girls had he slept with before?

It didn't matter, it really didn't.

I was ready.

I pulled up my skirt and wiggled out of my underwear. It wasn't nearly as graceful or as sexy as I'd pictured it in my head. "Condom?" I whispered in his ear.

"Oh, yeah," he said, kneeling up and reaching down into the back pocket of his shorts, which were on the ground now, around his ankles. He fished out his wallet, unfolded it and pulled out a square purple packet. I grabbed the waist of his boxers and tugged them down. He looked up at me, his face a mix of disbelief and total giddy joy.

Carefully, he tore off one edge of the packet, slipped the condom out and tossed the wrapper aside. I flashed briefly back to health class as he carefully rolled the condom down.

"You ready?" he whispered, as I lay back down.

"Uh-huh," I said, pulling him down with me, keeping my mouth on his. I kissed him hard and then it happened.

It hurt about as much as everybody said it would. And my butt was itchy, because apparently I hadn't realized we'd been sitting on an anthill the whole time. But the sun was going down and the eager moon was already out and the last strains of Grey Matters' set were pounding through the still, humid air, and it was amazing. Kind of. It was over pretty quickly.

When Shaun finally lay still on top of me and breathed out heavily, I smiled up at him. He rolled off and wrapped his arms around me, kissing my neck, my ears, my cheek and my forehead.

"Hey," he whispered, his voice, his eyes, his everything soft.

This fuzzy little bit of afterglow. Maybe this was what it was all about. This peaceful moment. This stillness. Minus the ants.

I didn't have long to think about it, though, because soon enough we heard voices, two of them, coming toward us.

"Shit!" I said, feeling around in the grass for where my underwear had landed. I smoothed down my skirt and jammed my shirt back over my head, backwards at first, while Shaun struggled to get rid of the condom and pull up his pants and underwear at the same time.

"I don't know," said a man's voice, "I think the worst of it is already over."

"It's just the timing's not right. And I'm sorry to have dragged you into all this." A woman's voice. Oh no.

"Do you hear that?" asked the man.

"Oh, Ken, don't bother …"

"Fuck!" I mouthed to Shaun, as he triumphantly zipped up his shorts.

*"What the hell?!"*

# Nineteen

"Jesus, Vic!"

"Mom!"

"What the —"

"Oh, god ..."

"I'm so, so sorry."

Our voices ping-ponged and ricocheted off one another and then out into the suddenly quiet night air, but Mom's voice rose above us all.

"What the hell are you doing?" she demanded. "I thought you were breaking up with this guy! Now I find you naked in the bushes? Honestly, Vic, what's going on?"

Oh no.

"You were, you were going ... you, wait, what?" Shaun looked, not surprisingly, impossibly bewildered by the situation.

Me: "I wasn't, I'm not —"

Shaun: "We weren't —"

Mom: "You didn't —"

Me: "We just —"

Ken: "Maybe we —"

Shaun turned to me. In his total shock, having only just made the connection. "Your mom is Micky Wayne?"

"She sure is," Mom said coldly.

"Look," I said, "can you just give us a second here?"

"Yeah," said Ken, desperately avoiding eye contact. "Maybe we should just go."

"Oh no," fumed Mom, "you two get your … your stuff together. We'll be waiting for you by that tree over there. You've got one minute." And then she and Ken stalked off.

Shaun and I were both standing up now, facing each other.

"What the hell was that?" Shaun whispered.

"That's her," I whispered back, trying to brace myself for the conversation to come.

"Your mom?"

"Yeah."

"— is Micky Wayne?"

"Haven't we covered this?"

"Why didn't you tell me?" he asked, his eyes practically bugging out of his head.

"For this exact reason!" I whisper-shouted. "Come on, let's get this over with."

Shaun followed behind me without another word.

When we found Mom and Ken, standing by a nearby tree, Mom was already sucking hard on a cigarette. She'd quit for good a few years ago, and it was the first time I'd seen her light up since then. She kept a tally in pencil on the inside of her closet of the number of days that she'd gone without a cigarette. She'd have to paint over it and start again.

"Okay," she said, dropping the cigarette to the ground and grinding it out with the toe of her cowboy boot. "You two," she pointed at Shaun and Ken, "get going. I don't care where. Ken, we'll talk later. Shaun?" She tried to soften her tone, but it didn't really work. "It was nice to meet you."

"Okay," said Ken, steering Shaun away from us.

Shaun looked back over his shoulder. "Uh, bye," he said, "It was, uh, nice to meet you, too."

But he wouldn't even meet my eye.

I couldn't imagine how awkward Ken and Shaun's conversation was going to be en route to wherever they were headed, but I knew it wouldn't be half as bad as what Mom had in store for me.

She was all dressed up for the show. The cowboy boots she'd had forever were matched with a sleeveless green vintage dress she'd bought in Kensington just before she left for Japan. Her hair was braided and done up and she had a lot more makeup on than usual but it looked good, like someone else had done it for her. She really did look like a rock star. A rock star who was about to murder me in cold blood.

"Let's take a walk," Mom said, forcing herself to breathe slowly.

I nodded, as if I had any choice in the matter, and followed her.

"So," she said, "Shaun. You didn't break up with him?"

"No," I said, looking down at the ground and kicking at a stray pebble in my path.

"You lied to me to keep me off your trail?"

"Uh-huh," I said. Sometimes she was so dead-on it was scary.

"And you just slept with him."

"Mmhmm."

"For the first time?" She stopped walking and looked me in the eye.

"Uh-huh," I said, swallowing the little bit of puke that had suddenly welled up in my throat.

"Oh, baby."

Suddenly her arms were around me in a hug so tight that it felt like it might have been some kind of punishment. And then, just as suddenly, she let go.

"You were safe? He used protection? He didn't pressure you?" Boom, boom, boom. Interrogation time.

"Yeah, yes, no, of course he didn't," I said. "I wanted to. We wanted to."

"Okay," she said, exhaling. "Okay."

She sat down on a bench lining the path and I took a seat beside her. She pulled out another cigarette from a pack she must have bought that morning and lit it, sucking hard and then exhaling smoke.

"You definitely win some kind of prize," she finally said. "Worst First Time Ever."

"You gonna make me a trophy?" I asked.

"Oh yeah," she said, fanning her smoke away from me, "an anatomically correct one."

"You're so gross," I said, joining in on the fanning. The wind kept blowing it right into my face.

"Says the girl whose butt is covered in ant bites."

252

"Mom!"

"What," she said, "it's true, isn't it?"

I slid my butt back and forth along the bench to scratch the bites that were already welling up under my shorts. "Maybe," I admitted. "But how did you know?"

"I'm not sure how exactly you missed seeing the giant anthill you guys were sitting on."

"I figured it out a bit too late," I said. "I guess we were kind of distracted."

"It's like they say — once bitten, twice shy."

"You are actually the worst person in the world," I said. "Ever. I hope you're aware of it."

"I most certainly am," she said, exhaling and then putting out her cigarette.

And just like that, we were back to where we'd started. Well, almost.

"I'm sorry," I said. "Sorry I ran out last night."

"You went over to Shaun's place, huh?" she asked.

"Uh-huh."

"And what did his parents think of that?"

"I met them this morning," I said. "They were pretty mad, I think, but it was okay. They made me breakfast."

"Wow," Mom said, "Shaun must've put in a good word for you."

"I guess."

"But you are not pulling this crap with me anymore, you understand? You're seventeen, not twenty-seven. Even if I sometimes forget."

I nodded.

"No more secrets," she said. "None. Okay?"

I nodded again.

"And I'm sorry, too," she said. "I know it hasn't been a great summer for me, you know, as a mom. But I really want to make it up to you, okay? I've been working extra shifts at the café, and I borrowed some money from your gran, and I think you should come with me to Europe. Six weeks on the road, we're going to see amazing things. We'll get you a tutor so you won't even have to miss much school."

Finally, finally, finally. Though it was kind of too late. I had my own life now, but that was all right. It was mostly just the thought that counted, anyway.

"That's all right," I said, "I think I'll stay. There's, you know, good stuff here."

"Yeah?" she said, like she wasn't sure she'd heard me right.

"Yeah," I said. "There's, like, one more thing that I didn't tell you."

"You didn't get a tattoo, did you?" Mom said, checking my arms and legs for evidence.

"You wish," I said. "It's nothing like that. See, Lucy and I made this game."

"What kind of game?" Mom asked.

"On her computer. It's pretty basic, but it turned out kind of cool. Anyway, we presented it to this group called She Shoots. They're this, like, feminist collective. They teach game-making and stuff. Anyway, Lucy and I want to go back and take some of their workshops and become actual members. They really liked us. It was pretty amazing."

"Wait a minute," Mom said, "She Shoots?"

"What," I said, "you've heard of them?"

"Of course," she said. "Sasha, the one who runs it? She comes by the café all the time. She's friends with Sal. I wish you'd told me you guys were going. I would have introduced you!"

I wasn't surprised at all that it turned out Mom had a She Shoots connection, but I was proud that Lucy and I had gone into it on our own.

"Nah," I said, "it was better this way. But anyway, that's how I met Ken."

"Right," she said, "now I get it. He said that he'd run into you at the space where he works."

"Yup," I said. "He just missed our presentation."

"Too bad. So how many people were there?" Mom asked. "You and Lucy just got up and talked about your game?"

"Yeah, it was pretty scary, but everyone there was really nice. There were, like, forty or fifty people there."

"Wow," she said, "I can't believe I missed it! Did it go okay?"

"Yeah," I said, "it did. Anyway, there'll be more games. Lucy and I are going to start our next project soon, and I'm going to illustrate it."

"You really love this, don't you?" Mom asked, studying the smile on my face.

"I think I might."

"So what's your next game going to be about, your saintly mother?"

"Easy," I said. "You better sign me up for one of their workshops first. So I can truly capture your beauty in pixel form."

"Well," Mom said, fluffing her hair, "if it's for a good cause."

"Naturally."

"Wow, sweets. That's … wow. I'm really proud of you. You know that, right?"

"Thanks, Mom," I said. "I know."

"But you're serious about Europe? Just think about it, okay? It'll be an amazing adventure. I know you've got lots going on here, but it's Europe, you know? It's *Europe*. We'll be playing all over. It's going to be amazing."

And she was right. When I stopped to think about it, she was offering me an unbelievable trip. But it would mean spending six weeks away from Shaun, and could we even afford the extra plane ticket and all the expenses?

"I'll think about it, okay?" I said. "Speaking of which, don't you have, like, an enormous show to play?"

Mom checked her phone. The screen was full of message notifications asking, I'm sure, where the hell she was. "Yeah," she said, clearly not in much of a hurry. "I guess we better go."

And we walked, hand in hand, along the path connecting Ward's to Centre Island, though eventually I forced her to pick up the pace.

As we got close enough that we could start to hear the rumblings of the crowd, I turned to her. "Sorry about the stuff with Ken," I said. "I mean, I don't like that you're dating him, but I guess I shouldn't have said what I said."

"Thank you," she said. "I know the timing's awful, but I really like him."

"The timing wasn't exactly my biggest concern."

"Yes, sweets, I know that. Anyway, I don't know what's happening. We might take a break or something. Things are going to get messy once the book comes out."

"Once you see what he's actually written about you?"

"I've read it," she said. "Well, most of it, anyway. His first draft. It's good, and his publisher's really happy with it. This could be big for me, you know?"

"Because it's going to give all the Dennis truthers more fuel?"

"He didn't write about that stuff," she said. "Those rumours. He wrote it exactly like I told it to him. That Dennis is gone."

"Oh," I said.

"Yeah."

"So you think it's going to, like, boost your career?"

"It might," she said. "We're talking about doing a big American tour in the spring. We'll be all over. I think things are finally starting to happen for me again."

"Yeah?" I said.

We were interrupted by the rising volume of the crowd as we checked in through the side gate of the stage, Mom flashing her Performer lanyard, and taking me under her arm as her plus-one.

"There's going to be a lot more touring," Mom said, as we weaved through the assembled gear and the stray band members heading to and from the stage.

"Good," I said. "Then maybe you won't walk in on me and Shaun the next time."

"I am gonna kill you," she said, just as one of the tech dudes grabbed her for a super-last-minute tune-up. "Now go on, you know the drill."

I walked ahead up to the side of the stage where a few familiar friends-and-family faces were gathered backstage, waiting for Mom to go on. Among them were Shaun and Ken, who couldn't have looked more relieved to see me. Well, Shaun, anyway. Ken was still a profound shade of red. And just behind Shaun, almost totally lost in his shadow, was Lucy. Oh no.

"Why the hell didn't you answer my texts?" Lucy said, pushing Shaun aside to get to me.

"I'm so, so, so sorry, Luce. Oh my god. I totally forgot."

"Were you ditching me or something?"

"I wasn't, I swear. My phone died!" I said, taking it out of my bag and waving it in front of her as evidence.

"Whatever," she said. "At least your mom still checks her phone."

"Look, I'm sorry, okay? It's been, like, the weirdest day of my life. I'll tell you about it tomorrow."

"If I'm still speaking to you," she said.

"Aw, come on," I said, "you can't resist my charms."

"Watch me."

"Uh, hey," Shaun said, coming over to talk to us when it was clear that our fight had died down. "So … we're really here?"

"It's one of the few perks of putting up with Victoria," Lucy said.

"It's a pretty good one," Shaun agreed.

"Um, Luce, this is Shaun," I said. "Shaun, this is my friend Lucy."

They exchanged a wave.

"So you guys do this a lot?" Shaun asked. "Hang backstage, I mean?"

"The novelty wears off after a while," Lucy assured him.

"I don't know," he said, his eyes big like a kid who'd just crossed through the gates at Disney World. "I don't think this could ever wear off. I mean, I know your mom's going to murder me and everything, but I gotta say, this is worth it."

"I'm sorry," I said to Shaun. "For lying, I mean. I just … I wanted you to like me for me, you know? My mom has a habit of bulldozing over my life. I mean I love her, but I can't just share her life forever."

"Yeah," Shaun said, "I mean, it is kinda weird."

"Weird-bad?" I asked, staring out at the sea of people fighting to get up close to the stage. To get up close enough to see my mom play.

"You're kidding, right?" Shaun said, turning to me. "This is definitely weird-good."

# Twenty

en minutes later Mom and her band took the stage. Another band called Falter would be playing after them, who definitely had a bigger draw, but the feral roar of the assembled mass made it sound like they were the only band in the world.

Shaun, Lucy, and I had snagged a spot just behind Jana's drum kit. Ken had grabbed some toilet paper from the porta-potty backstage, and we'd all stuffed some into our ears to keep from going completely deaf.

"How you guys doing?" Mom called out, waving like she was addressing a small group of close friends instead of a giant crowd of screaming fans. "You're lookin' good tonight, Toronto. You feelin' good?"

A few voices in the front row carried over the din.

"Feelin' great!"

"We love you, Micky!"

"Play 'Stranded in Daylight'!"

"That's good," Mom said, "real good. Thanks for having me out here. The bands today have been amazing, and I am so lucky to get to share this stage with so many talented musicians. It's been quite a day, hasn't it?"

And over the white noise of the crowd's screams, I started to think.

I thought about how I really needed to work on being a better friend to Lucy. It wasn't fair the way I'd put my relationship with Shaun ahead of my friendship with her all summer. I couldn't wait to spend more time with She Shoots, but I had to remember that Lucy was the reason why I'd found them in the first place. She was the reason why I'd found something that I might love, and that I might someday even be good at. She was the only one I'd shared my drawing with.

I knew the story that I wanted to tell. About a man who wakes up one morning in Mexico with no idea who he is. Who sets up a bar on the beach, adopts homeless dogs, and learns how to surf. I wasn't sure I had the words, but I could already picture the game in my head.

I thought about how I couldn't keep Shaun separate from the rest of my life anymore. He knew all of my secrets now, and as strange as it was to see those parts of my world that I'd fought so hard to keep apart suddenly collide, nothing had exploded so far. I knew that there'd be more fallout from the knowledge that yes, Micky Wayne was my mom. The conversation wasn't over yet, it had barely even started. But the impossible grin on his face as he looked out at the stage said it all.

I hoped that it wouldn't be too weird. I knew that once Mom and Shaun got to know each other — once she stopped plotting creative ways to kill him, that is

— she'd be just as crass and weird around him as she was around me. So I figured I'd let him enjoy this last sliver of a moment when he still thought my mom was the coolest person ever. Next to me, obviously.

Mostly, though, I thought about Mom. And how, as much of a mess as she was, Mom was just herself, nothing more and nothing less. And that's all she was ever going to be. We were different, fundamentally, and that was good, that was the way it was supposed to be. I didn't have to share her life. I couldn't. There wasn't room anymore.

Micky Wayne might not always have crowds of adoring fans screaming her name, but, as flawed as she was, she would always be my mom. And the fact that she wouldn't always be there when I needed her, that we'd have more birthdays apart and holidays with her away on the road, was a trade-off. She had more albums to record. She'd be tied up in the recording studio as soon as she got home from her European tour, I knew, and I wouldn't get to see her much for a while. She'd be up until all hours of the night, recording songs to win over new fans.

She didn't belong just to me; a part of her belonged to everyone. It was the sacrifice we made for our remarkable lives. And I hoped that it would always be worth it.

Jana counted out the band's first song, and I was brought instantly back to the moment.

The band started blasting through their set list, and the crowd frothed into a frenzy with the blurred faces of the pit pressing up against the barriers to sing along. I'd never seen that kind of reaction to one of Mom's solo shows. It was pretty wild. The crowd owned some part of her that I knew I never would.

"Thank you guys so much. Wow, thank you!" Mom said as they finished up her newest single, called 'Stay Home Forever.' The irony of which wasn't lost on me. "I want to play you guys an old song, if that's all right. You guys remember a band called Dusty Moon?"

The chorus of cheers and yeahs and all rights rippled its way from the back of the crowd to where we were backstage. Ken stood not far behind us, though he was thankfully without his notebook. I caught his eye and we nodded. I wasn't happy he was still here, but I was curious to see what he'd written. Maybe Mom was right about the book. We'd have to wait and see.

"I miss that band every day," Mom continued from the stage. "Dusty Moon was my first real family."

The crowd crowed its approval.

I was glad Gran wasn't here for this. Not that she would have come anyway, but still, it was definitely a slight.

"My first real family," she repeated, "and I miss that. I do. And I bet some of you miss that band, too."

Another wave of agreement crested over the crowd. Somehow it hadn't struck me before just how much Dusty Moon had meant to so many people. It was different actually seeing it.

"But that family kind of fell apart, as you guys know. But fortunately, out of the wreck of that family tree, I started to plant my own."

Oh god. She wouldn't.

"Vic, sweets, can you come out here, please?"

Dammit. Dammit, dammit, dammit, dammit, dammit.

One of the roadies grabbed me by the arm and started leading me when it was clear that I wasn't going to walk out under my own power. I clutched at Shaun's hand and dragged him with me as the roadie led us to stand right next to my mom at the front of the stage, where the row of lights that hung above us blotted out the massive sea of people that lay ahead of us. All I could see was the mic and Mom, with the hysterics of the crowd nearly drowning out my own heartbeat as it *kerthump-kerthumped-kerthumped* in my chest like it was about to make a break for it.

"This is my daughter, Victoria," Mom said, addressing the crowd. "Say hi, Vic."

I gave her the most vicious cut-eye I could manage. "Hi, Vic," I deadpanned into the mic.

"She's got her mom's sense of humour all right," Mom said. "Now Vic's got her boyfriend Shaun up here with her. She's nervous, isn't that cute? Hi, Shaun."

Mom waved at him, and Shaun waved stupidly back, his mouth all but hanging open as the crowd yelled back, "Hi, Shaun!"

"Now these two are probably going to kill me when I tell you that I may or may not have caught them in something of a … compromising position? Not half an hour before I was due up here on stage."

From either the heat of the lights or this death by humiliation, I was going to pass out, I knew it.

Mom turned to look at me then, and when she noticed how ghostly pale I was — I'd used up my blushing quota for a lifetime, apparently — she pulled her mouth away from the mic and said, "Sorry, sweets. I had to." Then, back into the mic, she said, "You two go on backstage. I'm sorry, okay? Bad joke."

Shaun had to push me back to where we'd been standing because I was still too stunned at Mom's trick to move.

"Yikes," Lucy said, after Shaun had hauled me safely backstage. "That was brutal."

"Aw, come on," Shaun whispered to me. "You think my parents wouldn't have done worse than that if they'd found us in the bushes? She's your mom, she embarrasses you, that's what she does."

"She's the worst," I barely managed to articulate. My hands were still shaking with adrenaline.

"I'm not arguing with you," he said. "But I don't think she's done yet." He gestured back out to where Mom stood.

"Okay," she said, "that wasn't very nice. And this is what Vic deals with every day, poor thing. So to make it up to her, I'm going to play a song I wrote back when she was just a little lima bean in my stomach. This one's called 'Little Love Song' and it's dedicated to my daughter, Vic. If she ever decides to speak to me again."

Mom tapped the time out with her foot, and they launched into it, a slow and sweet ballad. Shaun held my hand tight.

"I haven't met you yet," Mom sang, as the crowd's collective voice swelled to join her.

Mom used to sing that song for me when I was little and had trouble falling asleep. When there were too many words and thoughts and pictures in my head that wouldn't stop spinning around and let me rest. Nothing bad could happen, she said, and nothing bad could touch me if she just sang that song for me. It was a spell, she promised. A powerful charm.

And I watched as the crowd — it looked like almost everyone, but maybe it was just everyone at the front of the stage — sang with her. This song, this spell, that she'd written just for me.

That nothing bad could happen to me was a lie, I knew, but I wanted to believe it anyway.

Shaun squeezed my hand so tight that I thought my fingers might fall off, and I leaned into his chest.

Lucy laughed at us but then she smiled.

"I know I'm gonna love you," Mom sang, "whether I want to or not."

And for now, at least, that was enough.

# Acknowledgements

Thanks first of all to my amazing writers' group, who helped shape this story from its infancy. Vikki VanSickle and Laura Hughes, thank you for all the beers and book recommendations over the last two and a half years, and here's to many more.

To my family, immediate, extended, and honorary (including the Christians, of course), for your love, support, and dogged guerrilla marketing tactics. I am so lucky to have you all in my life.

I am humbled by and thankful to Jennie Faber and Dames Making Games, the Toronto organization that inspired She Shoots, for allowing me to share my work within their community and use DMG as inspiration. Dames Making Games is a not-for-profit feminist video game arts organization, working to make interactive storytelling accessible to those whose voices are often underrepresented. Please check out their work at http://dmg.to, and, if you're in town, be sure to attend one of their many events.

I'm forever indebted to my beta-readers: my internShipmate Michelle Petrie, and DMG community members Kaitlin Tremblay and Allison Meades. Thank you so much for sharing my excitement and for making sure this book didn't suck.

A big thanks to Sheila Barry for providing early feedback on the story, and to Shannon Whibbs for the editorial expertise that helped bring it all in to shore.

Thank you to the Ontario Arts Council, whose support through the Writers' Works in Progress and Writers' Reserve programs helped make this book possible, as well as the Toronto Arts Council for their support through the Grants to Writers program. Big thanks to Avril McMeekin, too, for editing the sample I submitted with my grant applications.

And, lastly, to the staff of the Pueblito-Manzanillo Writers' Retreat, where I finished writing my first draft and, a year later, furiously revised it — you really made me feel like family.

# MORE BOOKS FROM DUNDURN

**Since You've Been Gone**
Mary Jennifer Payne

Is it possible to outrun your past? Fifteen-year-old Edie Fraser and her mother, Sydney, have been trying to do just that for five years. Now, things have gone from bad to worse. Not only has Edie had to move to another new school — she's in a different country. Sydney promises her that this is their chance at a fresh start, and Edie does her best to adjust to life in London, England, despite being targeted by the school bully. But when Sydney goes out to work the night shift and doesn't come home, Edie is terrified that the past has finally caught up with them. Alone in a strange country, Edie is afraid to call the police for fear that she'll be sent back to her abusive father. Determined to find her mother but with no idea where to start, she must now face the most difficult decision of her life.

**Throwaway Girl**
Kristine Scarrow

Andy Burton knows a thing or two about survival. Since she was removed from her mother's home and placed in foster care when she was nine, she's had to deal with abuse, hunger, and homelessness. But now that she's eighteen, she's about to leave Haywood House, the group home for girls where she's lived for the past four years, and the closest thing to a real home she's ever known. Will Andy be able to carve out a better life for herself and find the happiness she is searching for?

**In Search of Sam**
Kristin Butcher

Raised by her mother, eighteen-year-old Dani Lancaster only had six weeks to get to know her father, Sam, before he lost his battle with cancer. It was long enough to love him, but not long enough to get to know him — especially since Sam didn't even know himself. Left on the doorstep of an elderly couple when he was just days old, and raised in a series of foster homes, Sam had no idea who his parents were or why they had abandoned him. Dani is determined to find out. With nothing more than an address book, an old letter, and a half-heart pendant to guide her, she sets out on a solo road trip that takes her deep into the foothills, to a long-forgotten town teeming with secrets and hopefully answers.

**Available at your favourite bookseller**

Visit us at

*Dundurn.com*
*@dundurnpress*
*Facebook.com/dundurnpress*
*Pinterest.com/dundurnpress*